WITNESS MY DEATH

The murder of a pregnant girl in a Welsh mining valley, and the subsequent arrest in what the police consider an open and shut case, was a double blow to Taliesin Rees, who had been the local doctor for many years. Both accused and victim were his patients. Despite the police view that the case was closed, Rees set himself to investigate the death of the girl who had made such a strong impression upon him. His enquiries led him into confrontation and deadly danger, as the corruption of man and nature in the valley took a dramatic and inexorable revenge.

WITNESS MY DEATH

by

Roy Lewis

Magna Large Print Books
Long Preston, North Yorkshire,
BD23 4ND, England.

British Library Cataloguing in Publication Data.

Lewis, Roy
    Witness my death.

    A catalogue record of this book is
    available from the British Library

    ISBN   978-0-7505-3817-6

First published in Great Britain in 1976 by The Crime Club

Copyright © Roy Lewis 1976

Cover illustration © Richard Nixon by arrangement with
Arcangel Images

The moral right of the author has been asserted

Published in Large Print 2014 by arrangement with
Roy Lewis

Magna Large Print is an imprint of Library Magna Books Ltd.

Printed and bound in Great Britain by
T.J. (International) Ltd., Cornwall, PL28 8RW

CHAPTER I

Taliesin Rees swivelled gently in his chair so that he was directly facing the young girl sitting at the other side of the desk. She was slim in the waist but her curves were such as to suggest she might spread extravagantly in middle age. Her hair was black, a deep jet, matched by the heavy dark eyebrows of a typical Southern Italian girl. She was very much like her mother, and Tal could remember when her mother had first come to the valley, speaking no English or Welsh, carrying out the engagement her own parents had arranged for her when she and her fiancé were but children. This girl, she was much like her mother in looks – she owed little to her father, who was a balding, heavy-jowled, second-generation Italian who had a thick Welsh accent and was more interested in billiards than ice-cream. But perhaps people came to his ice-cream parlour because he was Small Retailer (Wales) Billiards Champion. People ate ice-cream for the strangest of reasons.

5

'Well?' Barbara Porelli said defiantly.

Tal Rees said nothing for a moment. His mind was drifting along old pathways, sunny afternoons on a hillside above the dark, gaunt pit wheels, and he could remember a little girl in a blue pinafore, with jet black hair and deep brown eyes, but it was all so long ago. Even little girls grew up – little girls, especially, grew up.

'Do you feel it absolutely necessary to sleep with every man who wanders through your life?' Tal asked despondently.

'I *am* pregnant, then.'

'For the second time, to my knowledge. How many times you've managed to escape you haven't told me. But I suppose that's none of my business.'

'That's right,' Barbara Porelli said. 'It isn't your business, Dr Rees.'

'No, my business is just to do the butchery bit afterwards, isn't it? Look, Barbara, the last time you came to me I did what I could. I arranged the abortion, and I suggested you went on the Pill. Now for God's sake, *bach*, why didn't you keep on it?'

She lowered her lids sullenly, like a schoolgirl caught out in a minor indiscretion.

'It makes you fat. And I used to get these pains in my back. It was uncomfortable.'

6

'Not as uncomfortable as a pregnancy you don't want, girl.'

A short silence fell between them. The girl sat still, her hands placed demurely in her lap, her eyes cast down. She would be about twenty-two now, Tal calculated, though he hadn't checked on her file. And it was just over eighteen months since she had been aborted at the clinic.

'So what are you going to do now?' he asked.

She lifted an indifferent shoulder but did not look up.

'Do you want the baby?'

She made no answer.

'You can't expect to have it off with some sailor in Cardiff and then come back here to me to get rid of the child every time, girl. If you feel you've *got* to go to bed with every good-looking stranger you meet, all right, that's not my affair, but contraception is the answer to that problem, not abortion. What I want to know now is what you intend doing about the fact you're pregnant. Are you going to keep the baby? Are you going to start facing up to responsibilities?'

It was as though he were talking to a blank wall. The girl made no move, but sat staring down at the floor.

'Do you *know* who the father is?' Tal said, with deliberate scorn staining his tone. It worked; the girl's head came up, her dark eyes flashed as she stared at him.

'I know him,' she said. 'There's no call for that sort of talk, Dr Rees.'

'Isn't there? I'm getting no talk out of you, Barbara. I can guess why you came to me. It would have been easy enough to go to a doctor in Cardiff, impersonal like, and probably get what you want – if you could afford it. But you come here, because you want me to talk, isn't it? You want to drive out a little of the guilt, come to someone you've known for years, hope for words of comfort. But I'm telling you this can't go on, *bach*. It isn't the way, grabbing for a bit of happiness in bed with anyone–'

'Not like that, Dr Rees.'

'Then tell me what it was like! Or *is* like! I take it you're still seeing the boy?'

Her eyes seemed to blank out and she was no longer seeing him. She sat motionless, with the same kind of inward tension that he remembered seeing the last time she had come to his surgery, and he felt as helpless now as he had then.

'I take it he doesn't want to marry you, or you wouldn't be here now,' Tal said. 'But I

8

think you should consider it. Not for the old moral reasons, the *valley* reasons. Your mother and father won't know about this, of course; your mother would throw a blue fit, the last time was bad enough and you haven't cut away completely. But if you love this man, if you're carrying his child, you should consider–'

'I–'

Tal waited for her to continue the interruption but the words died on her lips. She was looking past him in space and time; there were devils of calculation dancing slowly in her eyes, and he had the odd feeling she had almost forgotten where she was.

'Look, go to the man,' Tal said. 'Talk it over with him. You're three months pregnant now; if he can and will look after you, there could be a quiet wedding in Cardiff and your mam and dad won't raise much dust once it's all done. I know they always had different plans for you, Barbara, and maybe you had different plans for yourself too, but you just can't go on the way you've been doing, can you?'

She shook her head. Her eyes cleared, but he had the impression that his words meant nothing to her. He continued to talk but she was barely listening.

'All I do know is that there's no question of

an abortion this time. Before, it was different. You'd had a miscarriage only months before you came to see me, and to carry that child would have constituted a danger to you. So I could square it with my conscience and my ethics to carry out an abortion. Not this time, though, Barbara. You're a healthy young girl, and there's no reason I can see why we shouldn't allow this pregnancy to go its full term. It's up to you to sort this out with your young man. Is ... is it anyone from the valley?'

She pursed her lips. 'I'll sort it out,' she said quietly.

'Nothing stupid, now.'

'I'll sort it out.'

Tal Rees stood up, warningly. 'Don't you go near Mrs Jenkins, mind. I'm not having any of that nonsense. If you end up in hospital with an infection I'll go straight to the police.'

Barbara Porelli smiled. 'Don't be silly, Dr Rees. I said I'd sort it out. Not with an abortion this time. All I want is some money to tide me over; after that I'll be able to manage. I don't need a man or anyone; just a little money. And he's got some money behind him. I think I can persuade him.'

'To marry you?'

She gave him a long, cool look. 'To give

me enough money to tide me over. I didn't say I wanted to get married, did I?'

He had known her for most of her twenty-two years and yet there was simply no way in which he could communicate with her at all.

Tal thought about it an hour later as he walked up the incline where trams had once trundled coal down to the valley floor. It was a sunny evening, and there was a blackbird singing high in the breathless calm that had settled over the mountainside, but Tal's mind was occupied with thoughts of Barbara Porelli.

He could think back to his own youth and puzzle about it: there were so many of his actions that were inexplicable in logical terms, so many decisions taken for trivial reasons. But now, in middle age, he could not remember that his young years had been troubled by the same basic inability to communicate that possessed young people now. He wondered whether his elders had felt the way he did now, and yet he suspected not. After all, society thirty years ago was more *ordered;* there were not so many questions remaining unanswered. Preoccupations lay nearer home and nearer the heart – they did not lie in distance, space and time as they did now. Perhaps that was why the young felt so disorientated – horizons had been pushed back, fundamental truths lost or ignored in a materialistic society, and the mind of the youngster could not cope with it all. The pressures were so much greater now, than they had been when Tal was young.

Barbara Porelli was a case in point. Her father had been born in the valley and had grown up in the local schools, but there had been enough of *his* father's background present in the family to lead to an insistence that he marry the child of an old Roman friend. Old Man Porelli had closed his café one summer, gone back with his family to Italy, and when he had returned to the narrow confines of the valley it had been with a young bride for his son.

And just one year later Barbara had been born.

There were two other children after her – both boys. The parents had lavished a certain pride upon them, but Barbara, as far as Tal could make out, had been restrained. She had been quiet enough as a child, and he could clearly remember her chubby legs twinkling along Lloyd Street, running to the local primary school in the mornings. He had seen her round face become beautiful in childhood and then in womanhood. And he had seen her eyes grow deep and thoughtful and the first signs of resentment had appeared in her mouth.

For Barbara was of a new generation, a century away from Italy. Her father closed the café, opened an ice-cream parlour, established a sales round and prospered, as his wife managed the shop and he played billiards in his satin waistcoat and black bow tie. But the restrictions engrained in Mrs Porelli had no echo in Barbara and her first demand had been that she leave school immediately after taking her O Levels. She'd done well at school, as far as Tal had heard, but the sixth form was not for her – there were too many restrictions there, as there were at home. So it had been out of school, down to Cardiff for a job, and then shortly afterwards, lodgings in Cardiff, away from parental influences.

And within two years she had come to Tal.

There had been defiance in the lift of her chin and recklessness in her dark brown eyes. She was coming to him because she knew him, trusted him, respected him, but she was not prepared to be brow-beaten or criticized. It was her life and her body. If she chose to use them in a way that satisfied her, that was her affair. But she had a problem, a physical problem. And it had led to Tal's agreeing that she should terminate the pregnancy.

He guessed that she had been no virgin when she left school; it would have been her way of showing her independence even then. At Cardiff there had been men, obviously enough; she had almost boasted to him that she had kept a tally up to a dozen and then lost interest in the numbers game. He was of the opinion that much of it was bravado, a 'searching for identity' in the cant phrase, but if the effect upon her character should have been shattering it wasn't. She remained a likeable, beautiful girl; independent but not hard; an individual, but not indifferent to people. A woman who wanted to stand alone and find herself, be herself, and when she found what she wanted it would be time to stop and take stock.

Like now.

Tal wondered whether she had indeed found something and was taking stock. Her defiance had been plain when he expressed shock that she was pregnant again after an abortion and a miscarriage. But there was a determination about her that suggested to him that she had reached the end of one of her roads, at least. She had reached a decision – she was going to 'sort it out' herself. But it involved her parents and that valley not at all; it was her decision, taken in isolation.

But Tal was worried. It was a weakness, and he knew it. One of the essentials of general practice in the valley was that a man should retain his own identity, remain divorced from the patients who came to his door. Every old widow, every bronchial man, every young woman in curlers complaining that her husband had torn her three miles from the bosom of her own family and consequently she couldn't sleep nights, had a story to tell, a complaint to make, a demand for involvement at close personal levels. It wasn't enough to live in the valley and treat people for their illnesses; they demanded capitulation. A doctor had to be one of them: a respected figure, a man to look up to, a person to whom old miners would doff a dai-cap, but one of them nevertheless, part of a community, trammelled by the roots of their all-embracing love. For it was truly based on love – Tal believed that.

But it was the kind of love that Barbara Porelli had rejected once, and twice, and it was the kind of life she had cut herself away from, as she had cut herself away from her mother's original background influences.

But when a young woman tore herself from family and environment, where did she find her values? Only in herself. Tal knew it and was anxious, for he had never torn away, even if his reasons for remaining in the valley had been limpet-like, searching for the security a familiar lifestyle could bring.

Barbara had torn away and was now suffering; Tal had tried, saw something of her independence as a reflection of the independence he had almost won years ago. But *he* had lost.

He did not want Barbara Porelli to lose.

The incline petered out at the cutting where a loose fall of shale, some fifteen years ago, had brought down the rock walls on to the old rusted line. There had been a bridge across that cutting and Tal had played there as a child, chased away by the angry old watchman with the evil reputation. It was said he kept adders in a box and let them bite him to increase his venom. And he got the adders from the mysterious grassy dip that Tal now skirted on his way across to the mountainside.

There was a light breeze up here. Ferns waved as he passed and he could see perhaps five miles down the twisting valley, through a light haze that owed little to nature – along the terraces wives kept fires in the grates even though summer was close. And yet times were changing radically. The pits were all quiet now, and the long backs of the inclines and the black tips were greening, as tough grass sprang out of the slack and nature claimed back her own. On the far hill, up towards Pen-Rhys, the serried ranks of small firs stood to attention in the ploughlines of the afforestation scheme that was changing the character of the mountainside, but on this slope where Tal now stood sheep still chewed complacently, wall-eyed at his approach.

Directly ahead of him was the golf course that Edward VIII had opened and bad drains had closed: the colliers had started to enjoy their golf for a few seasons in the 'thirties and then the bog water had seeped up, under the torrential rain and the ever-present mist. The walls of the golf club remained as a monument to a dead prince, but Tal was more concerned now with a different kind of monument. He turned aside at what had been the second green, climbed the short hill to the top of the bank and clambered down into the narrow cut, thirty feet wide, where the rivulet twisted across boulders and through alder roots. He followed the course of the stream up towards its source, then climbed the bank again, half a mile above. Around the great shoulder of the hill, and then he was on the old tram path again, and below him was the narrow cwm he had come to see.

But someone was there before him.

<h1 style="text-align:center">2</h1>

'Hello, Dr Rees.'

'Dai... Pimping again then, is it?'

'Tryin'. Waste of time it is, though. Time was when those ferns down there used to be wrigglin' with them, all fat fish entangled together in a net, strugglin' to free themselves when they realized they was caught. But you don't see much these days. I think they all do it in the back of cars, is that it?' Blackened teeth grimaced sadly at Tal. 'No pleasure left in a good walk any more. Only things you see on their backs these days is sheep. Time's changing, isn't it?'

He was just five feet two inches high, and he weighed little more than eight stone. His body was muscular and bowed, his legs almost lost in the baggy black trousers that he wore, hitched at the knees with leather straps, a relic of working days twenty years past. He was seventy years old and his face showed it, with his deep-set eyes, blue-scarred broken nose, and thin, bloodless lips. But his eyes belied his age – they were small and sharp and bright, full of the knowledge that fifty years of Workmen's Institute Library fiction had given them and the vision that watching the valley from the hill had produced. It was said that no one moved in the valley without his knowing; it was rumoured a man couldn't step outside his own front door and across his best friend's wife's without his being seen. He was sometimes called Dai Pimper, for his predilection towards watching the activities of the young courting couples in the long grass and among the ferns, but more often than not he was called Dai Ponies, for if there had been one love in his life it had been the blind shaggy beasts he had seen put down some twenty years ago.

It had been the kind of love that could still make a man sense the odour of horseflesh and barns, hay and fodder and droppings, about him. Or perhaps it was just that he hadn't washed in the last twenty years.

'What are you doing up here, Dr Rees? Only patients up here is in that level and they been beyond help these forty years.'

'I wanted a breath of air, Dai. And a look

at the cottages.'

'Aaah.' Dai Ponies cocked his head on one side, and scratched at his wizened cheek with a bony forefinger. 'I haven't been along there for a few weeks, but I heard that there was going to be trouble about it all. I'll come with you if you don't mind, Dr Rees, provided you don't give me any of that medical talk about how a man of my age ought to be in that bloody prison up at 'Ceiber. You won't get me in with the old dodderers till I'm on my back and sliding for eternity, you know.'

Tal smiled. 'I know. I've given up trying.' He waited while the old man creaked to his feet and braced himself on his bowed legs with the air of someone essaying a launch into the unknown. 'You still living up at the pit, then?'

'Don't know a better place,' Dai Ponies said, and stepped out beside Tal. 'It's dry, good roof, windows blocked up with sacking so the sun don't wake me in the morning, can have a fire when I want to and keep the door closed till I want to get out. Where's better? Not in that 'Ceiber place, I'm damn sure about that. Man's got no pride if he lives in a place like that. You tell the council *that* next time they send up some young insanitary officer to tell me where I ought to go. I showed him where *he* could go, I did.'

Tal grinned. Was it only the young who were so independent, when there were men like Dai Ponies sleeping rough for fifteen years on the hillside, to the chagrin of a reorganized local council?

He slowed his stride imperceptibly to allow Dai Ponies the triumph of knowing he could keep up with a man twenty years his junior. Dai whistled through his nostrils like a pony snorting under the harness: he even plodded like the animals he had cosseted in the darkness for years, head thrust forward, nodding, shoulders hunched as though heaving against the traces. Ahead of them a magpie rose in a flash of black and white, fluttering away in quick panic, as the incongruous pair made their way around the shoulder of the mountain to the rocky crag that gave them a clear view down into the cwm.

There were hundreds of these tiny cwms among the mountains. Some of them were watered by small chattering streams, bright now, but formerly blackened by seeping coal dust that emerged from the levels driven into the hillsides by old coal-owners, before nationalization closed the killing, uneconomic pits. And most of the cwms were alike in their configuration. A curving hillside, green and brown; ridges of rocky outcrop; high above, a cliff overhang where the steepness of the hill had crumbled under its own weight, and in the air a hushed murmuring that could have been insects or might be the faded whisper of life from the valley floor, borne high on the summer breeze.

But Cwmdare was different from most of the other cwms. To begin with it was larger. The ancient glacier that had torn out its shape had been deeper and wider than many in the area. Its long tongue had lapped down for almost two miles, and the grinding teeth of the ice had chewed away at the mountain to tear out a mile-wide chunk where it joined the main swing of the valley. But perhaps because of its size, Cwmdare was different on account of the use to which it had been put. A hundred years earlier the coal-owners had seen the cwm as a dumping area and as a work area also. Where other, smaller areas had been allowed to slumber on, quiet, warm, protected, scattered with rowan and alder and silver birch, this large cwm had been invaded by men with shovels and picks. Navigators had driven a line into the cwm, uncompromisingly straight through its heart, ignoring the curve and swing of the slopes. In the wider part a roadway had been built beside the railway line which would drag coal trucks up into the hill. Where the cwm began to narrow a small scattering of cottages had been built for workers. And high in the cwm itself the shaft of the Dare pit had been sunk.

The old records announced it had been a successful enterprise. The Dare had provided work for the men and money for the coal-owners. For thirty years it had prospered, and then had come one of those catastrophic periods when Cwmdare had become an evil word. A reputation had grown – to work in the Dare was to die. Pit falls, explosions, faulty propping, fire in the gobs, under-ground flooding, failure of winding gear, everything seemed to happen in the Dare. It had sat in the cwm, brooding like a great black malignant spider, a pithead that swal-lowed lives, and then at last in the 'thirties it had dealt its final blow. In one last, engulfing collapse, it had entombed twenty-five miners and the whole valley mourned. There was nothing other than mourning to do. The men were half a mile under the mountain; the fall was massive; rescue impossible. And faced by what was seen as sheer malignancy – though the mine surveyors reported that re-opening would be unprofitable as a coal-winning ven-ture in view of the high repair costs involved

– the coal-owners closed the Dare, and the colliers sought work higher up the valley.

The Dare was still there. Its reputation for evil dislike of man had lingered for fifty years, and there was still about Cwmdare the whispered hint of a shiver when children wandered along its slopes. But the years had taken away the basis of the reputation; the Dare itself was now old, and betraying its age. The stack had been levelled twenty years ago, the shaft where the fan wheel had driven air to workmen a hundred feet below was filled in and closed. The wheelhouse displayed the broken-backed dilapidation of an old man whose day has gone and who waits silently to disappear; ancient window-frames gaped mutely; here and there a piece of rail, rust-red, emerged from shale and grass to show the old line, and near the engine-house there were lengths of wire rope, torn open by childish hands for the core – cut into lengths and 'smoked' as pliant cigars by swaggering, penniless youngsters – and all the debris of an industrial past that was now little more than a memory. For the cwm had already begun to take its revenge on the Dare pit. Mountain ash had split the masonry, fern had spread a green carpet of fronds over the walls built against the hill. The harsh brick and iron lines were softened by nature, eradicated in many places, half-hidden in others. Half-buried boilers gave shelter to huddling sheep, an owl dwelt among the rafters of the decayed winding-house, bats flitted through the darkening windows at evening and foxes prowled the hill before travelling to fatter hunting grounds at the back of the valley terraces, for chickens and fat racing pigeons.

'My father worked in the Dare,' Dai Ponies muttered as they stared at the old pit, 'and it was rats he said was the trouble. He used to pick up his shirt after swingin' his pick at the face and they'd fall out of it, the rats. Used to go there for the warm, you know, and the sweat. Didn't work the Dare myself; the old dad wouldn't let me. Said I had to go up the valley to the Parc pit; safer.'

Tal had paused while the old man spoke, but now he walked on, Dai Ponies shuffling along just a pace behind him. The path curved around the shoulder of the hill, hiding the narrow neck of the cwm momentarily and then opening out again so that the men had a clear view right down the length of the narrow place to the valley below. It was a view that fascinated Tal; it was as though he was presented with the image of a battle. Man had raped the cwm, and now it sought to reassert its virtue, drawing about itself the tattered remnants of its green clothing, steadily progressing down towards the valley floor, greening over the upper slopes with the spoil ripped up from its heart a hundred feet below, covering the pithead with fern and moss and alder, breaking up the walls with frost and lush grass, sending a new spring bubbling out of the hillside to eat away at corroding iron. And it had succeeded for almost two-thirds of the length of the cwm – until it reached the narrow neck that lay as a spur across the first widening of the cwm.

There, it had been halted by two events. The first had been the decision of some stubborn old mining families to remain in Cwmdare, where their families had lived for sixty years. The huddle of cottages on the side of the hillside – there were eight of them in all – had resisted the creeping recovery of nature, and small allotments had been laid out, walls maintained, roadways, of a sort, repaired. The second event had been the ambitions of Tommy Elias.

Time had eroded the first of the events. The old miners'd died, the young sons had moved out into the valley, or down into the Vale, closer to Cardiff and work. The eight cottages were now uninhabited. But Tommy Elias was

26

another matter. Above the cottages, hanging on the hillside with a precarious, fingertip grip, was a slag-tip. It was perhaps the oldest in the cwm, dating back to the days when the Dare had first opened. It also made it the richest, for it'd been tipped in the days when methods of winning coal were less sophisticated and much of the slag was far from mere waste. During the years of the Depression miners had illegally picked over that tip, but they had only scraped at its surface. When years of plenty came, and the land never had it so good, the tough springy grass had begun to change the surface of the tip, making it as browny-green as the rest of the hillside. Nature was winning, until Tommy Elias came along. And he'd sent back the fingers of nature with great water pumps that tore at the tip, drove deep canyons into its side, stripped its head, dug gullies and pits, holes and chasms in a criss-crossing, interrelated series of channels that had as their prime objective the removal of coal and dust and slack for the powering of industrial furnaces and the aggrandizement of Tommy Elias.

The tip was scarred, black, exposed, its black gut ripped open to the sky, and now, true to the history of Cwmdare, ready to take its revenge.

27

'What do you think, Dai?'

'About the tip, or Tommy Elias?' Dai replied, and wheezed a hoarse old chuckle. 'Black as each other they are.'

'The tip.'

Tal folded his arms and stared down across the cwm as Dai Ponies shuffled forward beside him. He raised a thin arm, pointed with a finger that remained arthritically bent. His hand quivered slightly.

'I been on these mountains sixty years, up and down. Know these hills I do, and the tips as well. Tommy Elias shouldn't have had a carve at that tip, I tell you. Stupid, it was. That gully there, now, see it?'

Tal nodded. Elias had rebuilt the road that ran past the cottages to continue its curve up and around the hill in a sweeping S-bend above the cottages to reach the tip and then vanished. Its purpose was to enable Elias's lorries to trundle up, take on loads of slack and small coal, and rush back down the hillside to Treforest and the factory Elias had established to make industrial briquettes. To one side of the old tip pumping machinery had been installed. It was simple and direct in its application – brutally direct. Strong jets of water crumbled the ancient, binding coal;

28

the water seeped away, the mounds of slack were left. A mechanical loader dug into the heaps and piled them on the expectant lorries. But as the face of the tip had been gouged out the pumping machines had been forced to cut new channels – and the one Dai Ponies pointed out ran at an angle of forty-five degrees to the old cottages mounted on the hillside below them.

'It's going to cause trouble, that gully is.'

'That's the rumour.'

'Look up to the left-hand corner of that flat place, Dr Rees. See that sort of shiny bit, there?'

Tal shaded his eyes with his hand. The lower edge of the channel was fronted with a lip of shale that acted as a wall against the roadway running below it. Just above the lip the slack was piled in a long slope. As Dai Ponies stated, it shone with a dull blackness, and at the edge of the lip itself there was a glint as though the sun caught a bright surface.

'That shiny bit,' Dai Ponies said with a severe diagnostic precision, 'is water. *Saturated*, it is.' He appeared proud of the word, and repeated it. '*Sat*urated.'

'That glint below it, Dai. Is that water?'

'Aye. A sheet of it there is, I reckon. There'll

29

be some of it will have seeped through, see, and collected above the road. That's what I mean when I say there'll be trouble.'

'Tell me.'

Dai Ponies wrinkled his nose in satisfaction at being asked to expound his theories. 'Well, it's like this, Dr Rees. You could say it was a stupid place to build a tip in the first place, couldn't you, but that's how it was in the old days, I mean, they didn't *care,* did they? All they wanted to do was sink a pit, put up some cottages close by where the colliers wouldn't have far to go to work, and then when the work started, dump all the slag in the nearest place they could, to save money. So, because there'd have been a flat place just up behind those cottages they dumped there until it got too high to dump any more and then they went further down the cwm and began again. And all that raw slag, lumpy and hard, and bound with dust, it was safe enough really, I suppose, 'specially when all the grass began to tie its roots in it and bind the whole lot together.'

He rubbed a leathery wrist against the base of his nose and sniffed. He inspected the back of his hand, then rubbed it against his jacket.

'That's okay all that is, fifty years on. But if

a chap then comes along and starts to dig in the tip, you can expect things to change a bit, can't you? And when he's bloody stupid enough to say he's going to dig it with *water,* and the flamin' council is stupid enough and greedy enough not to stop him, what can you expect? Only trouble, Dr Rees! Trouble.'

Tal stared at the shining slope. 'You think that slope is full of water pumped in by Elias.'

'Didn't say that, Dr Rees.' Dai Ponies shook his head. 'No, damn, can't hold the man responsible for everything now, can you? But it's all *part* of it, you see: you know as well as I do how much rain we get here in the valley. Down there, in the winter, you see the drains full, water swirlin' to get down and away. Up here there's no drains, is there, except old ones. Got to say about the old tippers, they used to lay drains under these tips. If you look down there, now, just above the cottages and to the right you'll see the old brick culvert that used to wash away the rains from the tip. But seeing how it was broken to make the roadway? Another stupid thing, isn't it?'

'So that slope is saturated with rainwater that hasn't been able to seep away, and with the jets that Elias has pumped in. The thing is, Dai, is it dangerous?'

31

'The Dare pit was dangerous,' Dai Ponies said with a chuckle. 'The hills is dangerous in the darkness. Living is dangerous, isn't it, with death staring you in the face, and getting nearer every minute you pass by? But it all depends on what you mean, Dr Rees.'

Tal smiled. 'You know what I mean. That slope is full of water. The slack is holding it. We've had a sunny week, but it's still shining. You go up close to it and the shine goes, the earth is slippery, but binding. But from over here it shines. If we get heavy rain next week, or the week after, what's going to happen? Is that slope going to slide?'

'Well, there you are, then. Slide it will, Dr Rees. I'd bank on it, bet a thousand pounds on it I would, if I had the money, but if I did I wouldn't be here, would I? Thing is, you can walk on that slope right now and it doesn't shiver; nor will it ever, until the rain changes it. You see, it's not really a question of a slide at all. More rain, after those water jets, and the whole composition of that tip will change. I've seen it happen over the years. It just becomes a black slurry, like porridge you've put too much milk on, and there's no way you can hold that stuff. You can build walls, cut channels, set up barriers, but I tell you there's no way you can stop the stuff.

Bad, it is.' He squinted up at Tal wickedly. 'But dangerous, that's another word, isn't it?'

Tal made no reply and after a moment Dai Ponies gestured across to the cottages. 'No one living in those places, is there? So, dangerous?'

'They've recently been bought from the council,' Tal said softly.

'Aye, and bloody daft they were to buy them too!'

'It's a sound enough idea,' Tal said mildly. 'The Trust has as its objective the establishing of holiday cottages for deprived children, and Cwmdare is a perfect place. A wild mountain to ramble over; industrial archaeology to explore; an education into the ravages of industrial man and the compensatory influences of nature reclaiming her own. A perfect spot for young kids to enjoy themselves, Dai, and learn at the same time.'

Dai Ponies grunted. 'And die, too, if you put them in those cottages. This year, next year, them houses will get buried.'

'What if Elias stops work?'

'Tommy Elias stop making money? Like asking him to stop breathing, that is. I tell you, Dr Rees, I knew old Jack Elias Rest-Day. They used to call him that because he never took one. Worked every day, week in, week out. Down the pit six days, he was, pony and cart – nice little pony he was too – Sundays, pickin' up rag and bones around the streets and selling down Ponty every other Sunday. Never still, he wasn't; up and down, rushin' here and there, making a bob on this and a tanner on that. That was what it was all about, see – hard work and money. The work was like his blood to him: necessary. Money, that was like good health: enjoy having it but don't give it up. So he worked like one of them blackies, and he saved like money was the road to Jesus. And it was all there in his house, they said, when he died. Old pound notes, some of them useless – out of date, see – but he was clutchin' that old box when his lids turned up and Mrs Oban laid him out. But Tommy got his hands on the box before Mrs Oban got there so she never knew how much there was. She'd have known otherwise, of course. Now Tommy, he's like Old Jack. Takes *his* rest days he does, but he's got the same fevers as his father. Just he's cleverer; uses his head rather than his back, like Old Jack Elias did. Found out about corners, and how to cut them, you know. Same drives, but different way of handling them. So take it from me, nothing will persuade Tommy Elias to *stop* that work.'

'The Trust want to stop him.'

'Won't see the day.'

'The answer is compensation – build cottages further up the cwm.'

Dai Ponies began to shake with a laughter that was completely silent. But there was no privacy in the joke; Tal knew as well as Dai the opinion the valley had of the son it had spawned by the name of Tommy Elias. He had left the valley when he was eighteen and he had come back when he was thirty-five with a plan to make himself a million. There were some who said he was almost there – look at his house in Barry. There were others who said he could make money, but he couldn't hold it. But on one thing all were agreed. He was happy to spend his money on himself – but on others, never. He'd rather burn a pound than give it to a charity.

As for cottages on a hillside, what right did deprived children have to fresh air, anyway?

3

The surgery was a grey-stoned, three-storied house situated on the main road, backed by rising terraces of owner-occupied houses, faced by a Methodist chapel, fifty yards from a bus stop, eighty yards from a public house, one hundred yards from a greengrocer's and a fish and chip shop, and one hundred and twenty yards from a butcher's. It needed, Lyn Morgan thought wryly, only an undertaker's to constitute an almost completely self-contained community.

But what did *she* need to make herself a whole person? As she let herself into the surgery and walked through the consulting-room, the thought lingered in her mind. She looked about her at the pale green walls and remembered when they had been dark and brown; she saw the smart tables and the scattered magazines in the waiting-room, and she remembered the oilcloth on the floor, the oil burner bringing smoky warmth to the room, tattered copies of the *South Wales Echo* decorating the stiff-backed wooden chairs. She could look back to that long-ago time when she was five and eight and twelve years of age and she could see herself as a rounded, if immature person. But what was she now?

Thirty years of age, she thought grimly, that was certain. A pale face, black hair drawn back severely, making her jawline seem narrower than it was. All right, she could change her hairstyle, but she was always so busy here in the practice. And who would notice if she did? Tal wouldn't.

She took off her coat and inspected her face critically in the mirror in the hallway. Her eyes were dark blue in colour and, she knew, excitable enough to betray her feelings, but, she proudly thought, never her professional opinion. Good-looking enough, intelligent, well-educated, sharp-tongued when the occasion warranted, five feet seven inches tall with a waist that showed signs of thickening, she had attributes enough. Fred Thomas the librarian had thought so anyway, but his assets did not appeal to her. And Evan Ritchie thought so, even though his motives were transient. But all this she read in her mind and saw in her mirror told her little enough. She could remember the little girl and the impassioned teenager, but she could not see herself as a person now. Merely a collection of emotions lacking form; a mass of prejudices and opinions lacking direction; an articulate, committed, clever woman who was not a woman – at least, not the kind of woman she wanted to be.

For what Lyn Morgan really wanted out of life was–

She heard the door open beyond the hallway and she started guiltily from the mirror. Her professional face was smoothed on in an instant, and the soft helplessness she had seen in her own dreaming eyes a moment ago would now be replaced, she knew, by the competent, assured glance of Dr Lyn Morgan, junior partner in Taliesin Rees's practice. Tal'd come in and see it and recognize her in a way he would, perhaps, not recognize the girl she had seen in the mirror.

For that was the trouble with Tal. Pain had blinded him, hidden him behind a protective screen through which he saw only certain aspects of life with his disturbing clarity – those which came near home, and might touch him personally, these he could not see. It was a blindness of deliberation. She knew it. She could not tell whether Tal knew it.

'Lyn? Are you in there?'

'Yes, Tal. I've just come in. Where have you been?'

Tal walked past her, smiling slightly and raising a casual hand in greeting, to make his way into the small sitting-room beyond. 'You going to make a cup of tea?' he asked.

'Like always.'

She went into the kitchen and cleared away some of the mess of cups and plates while she waited for the kettle to boil. The thought was there in her mind, even though she tried doggedly to curb it. If she lived here, instead of simply working here, there wouldn't be this kind of mess in the kitchen. The kettle hissed at her, whistled; she removed it from the gas ring, heated the teapot, made the tea, washed several cups, placed three on a tray with a half-full sugar bowl and a small milk jug and carried the tray into the sitting-room. Tal was sprawled in the leather chair. His eyes followed her movements as she came in and set down the tray.

'Three cups?'

'You remember,' she said. 'Evan's coming in shortly. Partners' conference.'

'What about?' Tal asked.

'He'll tell you,' Lyn replied, not willing to let the unpleasantness seep into the room so soon. She could have a little while with Tal now, before Evan Ritchie arrived. There were not many occasions these days when she and Tal seemed to have time for a chat.

'Cwmdare,' Tal said as she poured him a cup of tea.

'What?'

'You asked me where I'd been. Walked up to Cwmdare. Had a look at the cottages, and the tip.'

Lyn finished pouring the tea, spooned in some sugar for Tal and then settled down with her own cup in the brocaded armchair

39

near the window. She sipped her tea, then put the cup down.

'What was it like?' she asked.

'Difficult to say. But I think the cottages are threatened all right. Heavy rain, and it could be all over for them.'

'So the Trust will have to keep the pressure on Mr Elias, then?'

'If they don't, they'll lose their investment,' Tal said grimly, 'and a lot of kids will lose a little happiness.'

'It's a shame,' Lyn said warmly. 'I was talking to the vicar's wife this morning and she was telling me the Trust has taken legal advice but it hasn't been very helpful. They've written lord knows how many times to Elias, but all they've had so far is curt refusals to do anything, or even talk about the matter. I just don't know how anyone can be so rude, and so insensitive.'

'He's all that, and more,' Tal said. 'At least, so Dai Ponies suggests.'

'How do you mean?'

Tal frowned. When he did so his heavy black eyebrows formed a straight ridge like a black bar, in startling contrast to the white thinning hair that he grew thick about his ears, sparse in top. 'Well, he wasn't very specific. But after we agreed that trying to get money out of Elias would be like taking his life blood, Dai got around to hinting that Elias knew too many people too well to be ever called upon to disgorge. In other words, friends in high – and not so high – places.'

Lyn pulled a wry face. 'The rumour is that the Trust paid about eighteen thousand pounds for those cottages–'

'The council charged them *that?*'

'Including the access and a little bit of land at the back of each cottage, which could be used to build an adventure playground. And they were going to throw in a construction team as well, Tal, to make sure drainage and all the rest was all right.'

It was Tal's turn to pull a wry face. 'Too many businessmen on that council,' he said.

'Anyway, the Trust are arguing that the option for Elias is to provide or buy another site for them, but they're getting little change out of him.'

'There is another alternative: he could stop work, and put to rights the mess he's made.'

Lyn sipped her tea and shook her head. 'I understand that'll cost him a damn sight more than eighteen thousand so he's not likely to adopt that course. No, I think the Trust are in for a long fight – and maybe a dirty one, too.'

'Well, *bach*, it's not one for us to get involved in.'

'Did the Trust approach you, Tal?'

'They did. But dammit, Lyn, I can't be the conscience of the valley! We've enough on our plate already, with the practice, and the Hospital Action Committee as well.'

There was an unwonted irritation in his tone, but Lyn guessed that the irritation was directed largely against himself. The reason why people approached Tal Rees to help them in their troubles was that he was a sympathetic man. They trusted him as their doctor, but the trust went deeper than that. To many he was a symbol, aid and advice and assistance categorized and epitomized in the glance of his soft brown eyes. He never sought to lead but found himself leading; he never sought to speak and yet found himself spokesman. He displayed no interest in politics or pressure groups and yet he was constantly being asked to join this or that committee. Some he refused, most he accepted. And the Hospital Action Committee had been one he felt he could not turn down, since as a project it lay close to his heart. The demands it had made on his time these last months had been severe, nevertheless, and she could understand that he would find it necessary to refuse to take on the Trust problems as well. And yet he felt guilty at opting out from those problems; he had gone up to Cwmdare today to look at the cottages because he felt he *should* be doing something about them. But time was his enemy.

But wasn't it an enemy to them all? she thought to herself, reflecting upon the scattering of grey hairs she was too proud to conceal. Or was it that she was trying to show Tal she was growing older? Like him, she was a confused welter of emotions, too.

'The meeting tomorrow night should bring about some results, anyway,' she said after a short silence.

Tal did not look at her. 'Why do you think that?' he asked.

'Evan told me he'd invited Ieuan James to come along and lend his weight to the argument.'

Tal frowned, and put down his cup. 'James... He's a catch for us, hey? But he's wading in shallow waters, isn't he?'

'He's got an interest, of course.'

Tal squinted at her wickedly. 'An emotional one, as an ex-valley boy, you mean?'

'No, a financial one. His firm has the contract for the construction of the hospital. It's common knowledge now. Not that it makes much difference to him where the hospital is built, I suppose, but I think he believes as we do – that the environment is there not to be spoiled.'

'Maybe... And you say he's coming up at Evan's request? What are we meeting Evan today for, anyway? You haven't told me yet.'

She hesitated, opened her mouth, then closed it again as she heard the front door open under the key which Tal had given Evan Ritchie. A trusting man, Tal, with his partners. Keys to his house. But no key to his heart. Yet...

Evan Ritchie came into the room purposefully. He did everything with an air of purpose, as though his every action was imbued with the dust of destiny. When he came into a room he seemed to be trying to fill it with his presence. It was not enough for him to *be* – he needed to be felt, wanted, admired, respected. The projection of his own image was an end in itself for him, a goal, and the image had to be large, immense – the great man on a great backcloth.

The valley and its society was not the right backcloth for him. His misfortune had been to be born into it. He and his sister had been brought up in the valley, because their father had owned the Llanllwch pit, and neither had enjoyed the experience – first, because the old man had been a tyrant, and second, because by sending them away periodically to school he had spoiled them for life in the valley. They had come to resent local people, and see them as small, interfering busybodies who wanted to know the insides of everyone's life. Evan's sister Diane had made the break easily after the old man died with debts eating up most of the capital arising from the decayed pit – she had married, divorced, married again and now lived in Yorkshire. Evan had tried to break away after taking his degree, but something had pulled him back to the valley. Lyn guessed it was an innate insecurity. He wanted fame: perhaps he could find it in the small pool between these hills. Today the valley; tomorrow the world, she thought cynically as she poured him a cup of tea now, and watched him accept it ill-humouredly, sip it with disdain. He wanted nothing from her at this moment, for he wished to maintain the fires of his anger and a cup of tea might douse them.

Tal leaned back in his chair, hands linked over his stomach, looking at Evan Ritchie benignly. 'Well, Evan, you had a good day?'

'No better nor worse than usual.'

'You look set for thunder. Is that why you wanted this consultation, to rumble a few black clouds together?'

Evan Ritchie glowered. He glanced towards Lyn briefly, then glared down towards his cup. 'It's a complaint I want to be aired.'

Tal raised his black eyebrows and grimaced at Lyn. He turned back to Evan. 'Complaint? About the partnership?'

'I'll put the facts to you,' Evan Ritchie said harshly. 'It's all a matter of ethics. It's about William Jones and his wife.'

'Willy Thatch,' Tal muttered, nodding. 'All right, what's the problem?'

Evan Ritchie launched himself into a background history that suggested neither Tal nor Lyn knew anything about the patient called William Jones who was known to all and sundry as Willy Thatch because he had once tried, years ago, to hide his baldness with a wig that had blown off and got caught in a neighbour's roof guttering. Both Tal and Lyn were silent, listening; both knew that such tirades were necessary to Evan, who needed to prove himself to himself, day in, day out, and during evenings too, Lyn thought, on occasions.

'William Jones is an example of all that is weak and spineless and vicious in our

46

society,' Ritchie said sharply. 'He is now in his mid-forties and it must be twenty years since he has worked a full week. When the pits were open he never worked more than a three-day week – it was a question of getting enough beer money to spend in the Alexandra Hotel and keep his wife and children from sheer starvation, and since the closure of the mines he's been concerned only with spending what money he could get from social security, and avoiding what work was offered him. Over the years he's come into this surgery time and again with the most trivial of trumped-up diseases and infections; he's taken us for fools and treated us accordingly; he's wheedled his way from one social security officer to another; he's bled the State white...'

Tal winked at Lyn, but she felt no fun bubble inside her at his appreciation of Evan's over-reaction. She knew what was coming.

'He's subsisted on charity for years; he's kept his wife short of money; he's spent most of what he's got in the pubs; he's occasionally resorted to begging in the streets; he's weak, cowardly, a parasite upon our society, and we have done little to curb the excesses of his nature. As you know, he's over six feet tall and built like a tank, yet he hasn't done a normal day's work for years. If there was one redeeming feature about the man I would grant it to him – but there isn't.'

'He's seeking an identity,' Tal said quietly. 'He's a coward who wants friends and has to buy them. A social coward, Evan. That's all. Not vicious. Everything else maybe, but not vicious.'

'Towards his wife he's vicious,' Evan Ritchie snapped.

Tal shrugged reluctantly. 'It depends how you look at these things.'

'I look at them coldly, not with your sentimentality, Tal! The fact is, he needs controlling. He's got eight children by that wife of his, and there's another on the way, now. It's ridiculous! Why the hell it should be allowed I can't understand! He should have been sterilized years ago – or *she* should!'

'They had every right to refuse,' Tal said mildly.

'As we have every right to refuse to abort!'

Tal frowned, glanced quickly at Lyn. 'I don't understand what you mean.'

'You'd better ask her.'

Lyn answered before Tal had time to ask. 'I've recommended that Mrs Jones's pregnancy be terminated.'

48

'Physical problems?' Tal asked.

Lyn shook her head. 'No. I reached the decision on social grounds.'

Ritchie snorted and the room fell silent. Tal was watching her, and there was something in his eyes she could not read. He seemed to be thinking of something else, perhaps turning over in his mind a distant conversation, or a recent one. 'You'd better explain,' he said at last.

Lyn swallowed, then said firmly, 'I appreciate that normally we discuss these cases together, as we agreed. I know the legal position, and I am aware of the dangers to which we expose ourselves in making these recommendations. But I felt unable to act otherwise. At the time I took the decision last week you were away, Tal, at that Cardiff conference, and I couldn't contact you. I felt it necessary to make the decision in the circumstances. I did not discuss the matter with Evan.'

'Why not?' Tal asked quietly.

'Because she knew I would not agree!' Ritchie interrupted. 'And I would not agree for the soundest of reasons – namely, there are no grounds upon which we can base such a recommendation.'

'There *are* grounds in my estimation,' Lyn

said stiffly. 'Willy Thatch has sired eight children; his wife is a strong woman physically, but emotionally she is near breaking point. They have a housing problem; they live in filthy overcrowded accommodation; the children are getting older and are ill-fed and ill-dressed; they are the butt of other children and other families; if this child were allowed to be born it could result in the breakdown of that home completely.'

Tal hesitated, his eyes fierce on her. 'It sounds slim, Lyn.'

'I stand by it.' Her voice rose a little, angry that Tal was questioning her judgment. 'I was of the professional opinion that Mrs Jones could suffer a physical and emotional breakdown if her pregnancy was not terminated. It could also result in the break-up of her marriage—'

'A lot of use that marriage is, anyway!' Ritchie scoffed.

'It's all she's got!' Lyn flashed at him angrily. 'And she needs our sympathy!'

'Sympathy is all right for those who can afford it,' Ritchie snapped back, 'but we can't. We're professional people with the power of life and death in our hands and we simply can't afford to let our minds be ruled by silly sentimentality. The facts of the matter are plain. We have an agreement in this partnership – if questions such as abortions arise we have to discuss the cases within the partnership. It's the only sensible way to protect ourselves.'

'Protect ourselves!' Lyn was really furious now and she felt the heat flood to her face as she leaned forward to confront Evan Ritchie. 'And who's going to protect Mrs Jones? The way I see things is different from the way you see them, Evan! For you, it's a matter of protecting a professional reputation, going by an out-dated rulebook drawn up by old men who have forgotten what it's like out there in the world of sickness and misery. I *know* what it's like, and I know what needs to be done. This is a social issue, dammit; we're not talking about a clinical situation that can be dealt with by reading up a textbook, or a law report, for that matter. We're talking about *people* not statistics, human beings not medical subjects!'

'But we're also talking about the law,' Ritchie insisted, 'and about professional judgment, and about professional *agreement*. I contend you've broken the rules in all three – by going to Salvatori in Cardiff for a second opinion, knowing damn well he'd go along with your view, you've broken the agreement

51

we made here in this practice; by taking the decision, I consider you've all but broken the letter of the law; and as for professional judgment, I contend that's gone out of the window entirely, because you're not concerned with the life that's started inside that woman's body – you're concerned only with the surrounding social circumstances as *you* see them. And I can't go along with that. I can't accept that such considerations, unsupported by *evidence*, should be relied upon to reach professional judgments. If I were to put the whole thing in a nutshell, you've shown all the worst traits that can be expected in a woman doctor!'

'Oh, hell, now we get the male chauvinist bit as well!' Lyn stared angrily at Evan's suffused face, and the sight of his own lack of control, his staring eyes and empurpled cheeks, caused her own anger to be checked. Deliberately, she looked away, reached for her cup and took a long, careful drink of tea. She replaced the cup with a hand still slightly shaking and she looked at Tal. He was watching her wordlessly. She knew he felt he had not yet received the explanation he was entitled to. She could not give it, not entirely, not in front of Evan.

'I'm sorry, Tal,' she said. 'Evan is right of

course – in part. I should have complied with our agreement. I should have consulted you both about the abortion. But you were away, and Evan is right when he says that I didn't want to discuss it with him alone for it would have resulted in disagreement. I didn't want that. So I phoned Salvatori.'

'It was wrong, Lyn,' Tal said softly.

'I know. But I have to be honest with you. I think I would behave the same way again in such circumstances. That woman needs help, Tal.'

Tal looked down to the floor contemplatively. He sat in silence for a while and then he glanced at Evan Ritchie.

'Evan?'

'Her motives were wrong,' he said stubbornly, 'and I can't condone the situation.'

Lyn felt an unreasoning surge of anger return to her veins at the self-righteous tone in Ritchie's voice. She turned on him waspishly. 'Oh, for God's sake, Evan, don't be so whiter than white! Don't say that your own motives are so undefiled. You'll be telling us next that you aren't in any way influenced by the outpourings of the Conservative League here in the valley!'

Ritchie's eyes turned hard and flinty. He fixed her with a glare that would have petrified a patient. 'Are you suggesting that my political aspirations are affecting my professional judgment?'

Lyn opened her mouth to make just that allegation but Tal forestalled her. He held up a hand, leaned forward in his chair. 'Now wait a minute. This ... ah ... discussion is getting out of hand. Let's just stop backbiting at each other. I think the allegation has been made by you, Evan, that Lyn had broken her agreement within the partnership. She admits this. I hope also she is prepared to apologize for it?'

Lyn hesitated, then nodded. She wanted to repeat that she would still not have behaved otherwise, but Tal wanted no more words from her.

'The other issues are matters of professional judgment, and Lyn is entitled to hers as we all are to our own, Evan. Now, the question is, can we not let the matter rest there?'

Ritchie shook his head coldly. 'I don't think we can. I'm sorry, Tal, but this issue is too important to be dealt with over a cup of tea. My considered view is that Lyn has broken our partnership agreement, and I don't feel that we can continue on the basis we have done.'

Tal was watching him carefully. He waited

for a few long seconds and then said, 'I take it you're suggesting we proceed further with this quarrel. Outside the partnership?'

Ritchie hesitated, glanced at Lyn; she knew what was in his mind. If this matter was taken outside, his own reputation in the community might suffer, with some people. And Evan Ritchie wanted to be loved by all who were influential.

'Not outside the partnership,' he said after a moment. 'Just inside it.'

'You're talking about dissolution,' Tal said.

'Or resignation.'

Something was happening to Lyn Morgan's heart. Its beat was unsteady, the blood pumping around in irregular spurts. And there was an odd feeling in her lower stomach, an ache, a desperation. She looked at Tal. His eyes remained fixed on Evan Ritchie. He said nothing for almost a minute. The clock on the mantelpiece ticked loudly in the silence and outside in the street a bus roared past, bound for the head of the valley. Tal slowly shook his head.

'So you feel that strongly,' he murmured, almost to himself. 'Well, we are all entitled to our feelings and our views... But I'd suggest, Evan, that we reach no hasty decisions. We must all consider this, sleep on it, perhaps discuss it further. We three have worked together harmoniously for several years. I'd be reluctant to see the partnership break up. I'm sure we all would. So … let's consider it coolly. Do you both agree? Let it slide for a few days, then if you still feel so strongly, Evan, we must talk again. You agree?'

Ritchie's fingers were tightly linked together. He glanced at Lyn, then nodded.

'Lyn?' Tal asked.

'I agree,' she said, but the beat of her heart was still irregular.

Tal sighed, picked up the teapot and poured himself another cup of tea. He managed a smile at them both but they remained stiff. Tal decided to change the subject.

'I was telling Lyn I went to look at the Trust cottages in Cwmdare. There's bound to be trouble there – and Elias is being stubborn.'

'So I hear,' Ritchie said. The roughness was fading from his voice as he brought himself under control. 'But I don't think we can afford to get tangled up in *that* affair. We've enough to do with the Hospital Action Committee. You're both coming to the meeting tomorrow night?'

Lyn looked up, nodded without speaking.

Tal cleared his throat. 'I understand you're inviting Ieuan James to the meeting.'

A glimmer of satisfaction appeared in Evan Ritchie's eyes. He smirked. 'I managed to persuade him. He's got an interest in the hospital, of course, in that his design has been accepted for it, and he's arranged the building tenders and all that. But he's pretty busy, not least because I understand he's involved in a legal wrangle over some constructions built two years ago with high alumina cement. He tells me the employers are trying to hold him responsible – though he assures me he was acting only within acceptable limits at the time – and there's a hell of a lot of money involved. I think we're very fortunate that he's agreed to come along to the meeting at all; he's pretty well known, has contacts with important people in the Vale and up at Westminster too, I believe. In my view, he'll be a useful chap to help us in our campaign.'

'I'm sure he will,' Lyn said, 'he's well enough known, after all, as an architect – though I'm not sure that in his building programmes he's ever shown much of a concern for the environment.'

She had meant it to be taken lightly, but when Evan looked sharply at her she guessed he thought she was still trying to attack him. She met his glance, and after a momentary hesitation, he accepted the remark at face value.

'Well, I wouldn't go along with some of his architectural monstrosities myself,' he admitted. 'I mean, some of those crematoria he built in America! But the fact is, he's a name, he knows all sorts of important people, he can pull some political strings, he reckons, and he's got credibility. I mean, he's from the valley originally, though he left for Cardiff when he was twelve. His grandmother lived in Lloyd Street until three or four years ago, though, and he used to visit her regularly at one time. She had a bit of money too, though you'd never have guessed, to see the terrace house she lived in.'

'How did you contact him?' Tal asked.

'Well, I happened to hear he was coming up again this week, in connection with the hospital designs, to talk to the council. So I gave him a ring. I mean, I knew him well once, of course.'

'That's what I mean,' Tal said thoughtfully. 'I would have assumed contact between you would have ceased in the circumstances.'

Evan looked at his hands and grimaced. He shrugged. 'Depends how you look at things, Tal. Water under bridges, is one way. But there's more to it than that, too. All right,

58

Ieuan James married my sister Diane and they got divorced after a pretty hairy scandal in the newspapers. And I've not seen much of Ieuan since then. But you've got to remember a couple of other things, too, First, I haven't seen my sister for years either, and when we did meet she always had her nails unsheathed. I never had any deep regard for Diane. The way I look at it, she tried often enough to kick my crotch and sometimes succeeded; when she tried to kick Ieuan's he twisted her leg off – metaphorically speaking, of course. Diane was a bitch, and still is, probably. Yorkshire is welcome to her. It's true that after the divorce I didn't see much of Ieuan, but, after all, he's been busy making a name for himself in his profession, travelling abroad, all that sort of thing. The fact remains – I've always got on well enough with him, and just because he and my sister split up is no reason for the end of my friendship with him. Anyway, that's the way things have been, and I'm sure he can be useful and helpful to the Hospital Action Committee.'

And to Evan Ritchie, Lyn thought cynically. If Tal thought the same it did not appear in his face.

'I'm not convinced he can be the man for us,' Tal said doubtfully. 'I mean, this is a *local* issue, a fight between the environmental group and the council. Do we want big battalions involved?'

'It's how wars are won,' Evan said sententiously. 'Anyway, I'd better make a move. I'm meeting Ieuan this evening, and he's staying overnight with me – he's got a meeting with some of the planning committee in the morning. And he's now agreed to stay on for the evening meeting of the Hospital Action Committee. So, I'll be off.'

He rose to his feet – tall, masculine, assertive, handsome – and looked at each of them in turn. The politician in him emerged, the man who wanted to be all things to all people. 'We'll talk again,' he said, 'as we agreed. But I ... I'm sorry I blew my top a bit. I haven't changed my mind, my opinion remains the same, but I just want to say, Lyn, that I am not rancorous about this. I don't want unpleasantness. I'd like this thing to be settled quietly and amicably – and, I hope, not hurtfully. I'll see myself out, Tal; see you both in the morning...'

After the door banged behind Evan, Tal put his head back on the leather chair and looked at Lyn. She met his gaze steadily. Nothing was said, but she felt as though sympathy and warmth flowed from his eyes, a beam of sunlight touching her, playing over her. She knew the feeling, had experienced it before – once, years ago, when she had first visited his surgery, and several times after that when she had been troubled, needed advice. But he had never said much to her on these occasions; perhaps he had not needed to.

'Well, Lyn, there it is.'

She made no reply.

'When he talks of resignation, he means yours,' Tal continued. 'And when he says he hopes things will be settled quietly and amicably, he means he hopes you won't kick and scream about being bought out and all that.'

'He wants no noise of any sort,' Lyn said bitterly, 'because that might upset his political ambitions.'

'Oh, come on, Lyn, you don't mean–'

'I mean exactly what I say,' she interrupted. 'You know Evan as well as I do. He's what … thirty-two now? A bachelor with rugged features of *Woman's Own* illustrations, and the desire to be a man of his time. You're as much aware as I am of his ambition. He's already got a seat on the council, which is something in itself for a man of Conservative leanings in the valley, but his ambitions go beyond that. He wants a Parliamentary seat, and he'll stand at the next General Election if he can get the local party to back him. He knows he'll get hammered, and will win few votes against Labour and Welsh Nationalist voting patterns, but he doesn't see his future in the valley at all. No, a good showing here and he'll be looking for a sounder candidacy elsewhere, where he'll stand a reasonable chance of success. But to get a reasonable showing here he has to impress people, not people like Willy Thatch and his wife, but the farmers and the environmentalists, the professional classes and the shopkeepers. He's not kicking about me because I've made a wrong decision; he's afraid of the Conservative League and its anti-abortion stand in the valley. But what's that got to do with life?'

'You're hard on him, Lyn.'

'Because I read him. He wants a theme to fight for and the Hospital Action Committee gives him one. He doesn't want to be tarred with controversy so he wants no abortion arguments. A clean practice; a resounding cause. That's what Evan wants locally. After that, he sees the road stretching ahead for him – to power.'

Tal sighed and shook his head. 'Problems never come singly, do they, *bach*? You faced your problem with Mrs Jones; I had my own worry with a girl today. She came into the surgery, pregnant again.'

'Is she after an abortion too?'

'I don't know what she's after. Barbara Porelli... She worried me. I feel I ought to be doing something more positive for her... I feel the same way about the Trust cottages, you know? Coming up the same time as the hospital business, I haven't time, but I feel I *ought* to be doing some thing. I'm getting old, that's the problem.'

'Rubbish.'

The sharp vehemence in her tone made Tal smile.

'Got to believe it, I have. I walk up to Cwmdare and I can tell you my lungs were lifting a bit. I'm fifty, Lyn, even though I forget it from time to time and feel different.'

'You dwell too much on how old you are,' Lyn said. She was unable to keep the warmth out of her voice. To her, Tal was the same man she had seen seven years ago, when she was a young girl in his surgery. He was thicker about the waist, his hair was thinner and almost white, in sharp contrast to his black brows, and there were lines about his eyes and his mouth that would not have been there fifteen years ago. But essentially he was the same person, and she could not accept that the passing of years could change how a woman felt about a man. Perhaps something of her thoughts was communicated to Tal, for his eyes clouded and he looked away.

'Evan … he was right, you know, Lyn. You should not have gone ahead, contacting Salvatori in Cardiff.'

'He was right about consultation,' Lyn admitted. 'I am right about Willy Thatch's wife. And you know what I'm trying to do, Tal. I'm trying to save a family.'

'That may be–'

'Essentially, would you have had me be subject to *other* emotions?'

'You're avoiding the essential point,' Tal argued.

'I can't accept that.'

'Lyn–'

'It was you taught me, *you!*' she insisted. 'When I came out of Cardiff Medical School and returned to the valley to begin practice, it was you who first told me that medicine was about people, not illness. It isn't enough merely to control a disease, you said; it isn't enough to cut out a cancer, to stuff pills down a person's throat, to operate, advise, cure physical ills. You stressed to me that the essential part of medicine, if not its very whole, is to recognize that you're dealing with a man, a woman, a child. I must recognize that they are people and not medical statistics; realize they hurt emotionally as well as physically. You told me to look upon myself as a healer of relationships as well as bodies – that it was as important to hold a widow's hand or kiss a spastic girl as to save a life with a flick of a scalpel. You told me it wasn't enough to prescribe – I should *feel* for people and know them. That's what you told me, Tal, when I was twenty-two. I've never forgotten that little homily you gave me. It was here in this surgery. I've not forgotten it. And I'll never stop putting it into practice.'

Tal smiled and looked wistful, as though he wished the innocence of his own beliefs were still as strong. 'You're hoisting me with my own petard,' he said.

'No. I'm simply reminding you of what you used to see as the truth in life. There was a time when you saw such things very clearly, Tal; clearly enough to inspire other people. I'm just refreshing your memory. And explaining my own conduct. For, in fact, you don't think I was wrong, do you, Tal?'

He made no reply, but sat there, refusing to look at her. When he raised his head at last he seemed deep in thought. Lyn waited for a moment, then put out a hand, touched his briefly.

'Tell me. If it had been you Mrs Jones had seen. If she had brought her troubles to you, Tal. What would *you* have said to her?'

Tal made no reply, but sat looking at her. She felt his thoughts were turned inward; perhaps he was looking back to the time of his own youth, when his ideals were clear.

The years had driven inroads into his character, the pain of the death of his wife, his immersion in the valley practice, his total commitment to a life in this community, these had all been factors in the creation of the warm, human, sympathetic person that was Taliesin Rees. He was a sounding-board for other people's anxieties and pain and he had taught her to be the same. But while they were close, they had never achieved the closeness she really wanted. Tal suspected what she wanted, even if he didn't *know*, but she thought he resisted it. Now, under the pressure that would build up with Evan's insistence that the partnership consider breaking up, there was the possibility that Tal might have to face the truth that lay in her eyes when she looked at him. It could be that thought which now made him look inwards; or perhaps it was simply that he thought she had been wrong about Willy Thatch's wife, and was too fond of her to tell her so.

Either way, she felt she – and Tal – had come to a crossroads. External problems pressed in on them as they always would. But if Evan Ritchie wanted her to resign from the partnership, she would. It would be Tal's watershed; perhaps it might even be a good thing, in that it could resolve for them something that might otherwise never be resolved, until Tal was dead and she was too old.

Too old to care.

She never wanted to be that old.

CHAPTER II

The Workmen's Institute was in many ways an anachronism. It was a tall, gaunt, Victorian building whose blank windows stared out over a valley floor littered with old sidings where coal trucks had once trundled, a football pitch whose leaky stand had never been filled since the club gave up the Welsh League ghost, a regimented pattern of terrace houses that were uniform in shape, colour and social class, and it gave the impression that it was a monument to those lively days of the past when the valley had lived and breathed coal, and when the building itself had been firmly in social context – the centre of activity, with the chapel next door, the hub of the town.

But now much was different. The small cinema which lay in its gut was used for bingo sessions; the debating hall on the first floor was gathering dust and memories; the games rooms where old men had played chess and dominoes year in, year out, were inhabited with broken chairs and rickety tables; and only the billiards room in the basement and three of the grander committee rooms on the top floor clung to a vestige of usefulness. Times had changed, men had changed, the Institute was no longer a haven for miners relaxing from their wives. Now, wives went out with their men, and the rooms of the Institute sighed and echoed.

In many ways it was a curious place for the Hospital Action Committee to meet. Tal suspected that it was a deliberate choice on Evan Ritchie's part, however: the meeting might be composed largely of middle-class professional people, but Evan wanted also to impress the journalists from the local *Leader* that the roots of the protest lay clearly in the community. And how better could he show that than by calling the meeting in the top room of the Workmen's Institute? The odd thing was that though no one was fooled, all went along gladly with the deception. Perhaps it was because they remembered the past and were secretly ashamed of their desertion of it.

There was a good turnout, anyway. Apart from himself and Lyn and the two journalists in the corner, there were perhaps forty other people in the room. Evan had taken the chair, for this was to be more than a mere committee meeting tonight, in that he had invited many of the more influential people in the valley to come along. It was in the nature of a general discussion about the problem of the building of the hospital and this gave Evan the opportunity to make a speech. It was all familiar ground to most people in the room, but Tal had to admit that Evan made the most of it as he spoke. He managed to inject passion into the story of events, and Tal was aware that the feeling in the room grew warmer under Evan's demagogy.

Evan started by describing the original plan for the Llandarog Hospital. It went back twenty years and had been beset by siting problems from the first. But in 1967 it had been decided that the new hospital should be built – to serve an area for twenty miles around – and the Area Health Authority had agreed to the plans. Tenders had been called for – and at this point heads turned to look at Ieuan James, sitting in the front row – and a bid had been accepted. Then, in 1972, the bombshell had burst. Planning permission by the local planning authority had been held up; the situation was to be reviewed, in the light of the projected new road that was to be cut in a wide swathe along the Pont Newydd side of the valley, driving through the hill and linking up with the new duel carriageway to Cardiff.

'Now, it's no secret what lies behind this plan,' Evan Ritchie said passionately. 'Let us be clear what it is all about. If there are to be any benefits to the people of this valley, they have escaped me, for they are minimal, to say the least. To the north of us there lies a new steel plant; while they close down the plant in West Wales they contemplate refurbishing the plant over the hill. All right, I do not question the economic reality – or absurdity – of that decision. But it is to link *that* works, and the feeder industries to the east of the valley, with Cardiff and Bristol, that this road is to be built. It has nothing to do with this valley. For us it means simply that lorries will roar through with heavy loads and choking fumes, along the side of the hill and through the valley, and for this they will be slicing the heart out of the place. For we all know what the project will mean in terms of clearance. Forty houses will be lost at Powys village; ten at Edwardstown. We are assured that there will be a reallocation of council houses to make up for the shortfall but we have heard those kind of promises before...'

He expounded at length on such promises. Tal's attention wandered and he glanced around the room. He knew most of the people here – shopkeepers, a scattering of councillors, three or four farmers who would be affected by the new road project. No one new, really; no fresh converts. Yet it was an important issue.

'Still, I'll dwell on these matters no longer, for what we are really concerned about is that an environmental issue arises. It is based upon two fronts. First, there is the fact that the quality of life in the valley will be affected by this ridiculous plan. We don't *want* all those lorries thundering through our valley! But second, there's the hospital. If this road project is allowed to go through it means that the hospital project must be put back for another five years, and a resiting must take place. The site has not yet even been chosen, though various ridiculous suggestions have been made – Bedw, for instance!'

A sigh of discontent rippled through the audience.

'Or Brechfa!'

There was an audible groan.

'Or even Cwm-ffrwd, of all places!'

Now several people moaned their displeasure.

'But let us assume they do put the hospital project back five years. Let us assume it is sited elsewhere – though I hope more suitably than at the places mentioned. What then is to happen to Llandarog House? I do not need to tell any of you what the plans for the hospital were. It was to be sited in a pocket of outstanding natural beauty and of historical importance! We have here in the valley, in Llandarog House, a place where our past and our heritage is buried. The D'Arcy family built that house, but though they came as strangers they stayed to become of us. They were the greatest and most philanthropic coal-owners in Wales. They created that hillside, where the trees of the park rival the days that have gone when woods clothed the whole of these valley hills. And when the family left, Llandarog House, and its park, was given to the valley. And we created something new there – an international study centre, where young people of all nationalities could come for six weeks at a time and live and work together. It was in those grounds, behind Llandarog House, that the hospital was to be built. It was to provide a sanctuary, a green setting where people could be nursed back to health. But what is to happen now? Llandarog will go, have no doubt about it! They *say* the road will merely skirt the park, but have you never seen road construction going on? I say they'll destroy the park; peace will go; birds will no longer sing on that hill; we'll just hear noisome lorries, choke from fumes – and there'll be no hospital to go to for treatment! For if it can be put off for another five years, why not fifty?'

Tal looked at Lyn. She smiled at him.

'He's going well,' she said, 'and the *Leader* is taking it down word for word.'

Tal nodded, and directed his attention back towards Evan. He was well into his stride now as the arguments poured forth. He had caught his audience, they were with him, listening closely, but suddenly Tal felt puzzlement creep over him. The tenor of the argument was changing. Up to this point it had been closely, logically argued, the presentation of cold facts in an emotional setting. But some other ingredient was being added, a new ingredient that was unfamiliar. Tal looked at Lyn and saw that she too had noticed. A small frown was visible on her brow as she listened.

The tone of Evan's speech had become accusatory.

'So these are the questions I think we should ask! First, what is the membership of the Area Health Authority, the membership which would seem to be bowing meekly to the demands of the Road Project Committee? Second, what is the membership of the local planning committee, and what was the voting pattern in that committee six months ago, three months ago, and last week? Thirdly, since Llandarog House is a listed building, what representations have been made to the Secretary of State, and by whom, concerning its future? And finally, at what point of time are we to be presented with a true account of the machinations that go on behind the scenes in our reorganized local planning structure, with the names of those individuals who first espouse causes so fervently and then when the time for voting comes turn coat and argue a case opposite to the one they formerly held?'

The Pressman from the *Leader* was scribbling furiously.

When the congratulations and promises of action and pressure were over, and the journalists had gone, Tal took Lyn by the elbow and steered her towards the door where Evan stood, slightly flushed, rather excited, and very proud of himself.

'Well done, Evan,' Tal said drily. 'I think you've stirred up a bit of a hornet's nest.'

'It's what we wanted, isn't it?' Evan said. Tal was about to query that, and the later remarks that Evan had made, when Evan turned aside to the tall fair man who stood beside him. 'Tal, I don't know whether you actually know Ieuan James.'

'I think we have met once or twice,' Tal said and extended his hand.

'Cut knees, more years ago than I care to remember, really,' Ieuan James said, and shook Tal's hand.

He was about thirty-five years old now, taller than the average Welshman, with fair hair and blue eyes that gave him a Scandinavian look, the Viking pillager of the North, power, muscle, drive. His skin was tanned, his teeth good. He gave an impression of cleanshaven wholesomeness that was nevertheless superficial; Tal felt that the surface charm covered an ambitious unscrupulous heart. He had heard it said that Ieuan James was a man of talents; he could have played centre for Cardiff if he hadn't valued his good looks and his hands – he had slender, tapering fingers and a keen brain and they could have taken him to music or medicine, but his creativity had exploded into architecture. And an explosion of a kind it had been too. His rise had been rapid. He had qualified as an architect in 1955 and won an award for a community living scheme in 1957. In 1958 he had received his first commission for a crematorium and thereafter he had branched out quickly into public buildings. In 1965 he had gone to the United States and opened an exhibition there, set up two subsidiary companies and generally had himself a good time. Perhaps too good, however; his marriage had crumbled, his American companies had been wound up, he had returned home to more mundane commissions and latterly had started to build up his contacts in South Wales again, from a large house and a sumptuous office in Penarth. He was rumoured to have won an important contract in the Midlands within the last few months; his contract for the hospital was long-standing, and was worth perhaps £50,000.

'I don't think Dr Morgan ever treated your knees,' Tal said, and introduced James to Lyn. Ieuan James's eyes lit up; he was appreciative of female company and if Lyn was a bit formal in her appearance she had a warm smile. As James engaged her in conversation, Tal said to Evan Ritchie, 'That was a bit of a shift you made in your speech.'

'Shift?'

'You started throwing out all sorts of hints. About the planning committee.'

Evan's eyes clouded. 'Oh, that,' he muttered. 'Well, that sort of came up at the last minute, I didn't have time to discuss it with you, but I'll explain later on. Look, Tal, I've got a bit of a problem. I had a call just before I left for this meeting – it's that Midgely case up in Pont Newydd. I think I'd better call to see him.'

'What about James? I could take the call for you, if you like.'

'Well, that's the problem,' Evan said hastily. 'Ieuan, I mean. It's what – seven-fifteen now? I think it would be a good idea if you could take him for a drink before he makes his way back to Penarth, or even dinner maybe. But I'd better get along to Midgely. Would you mind looking after Ieuan, Tal?'

Tal smiled, glanced towards James charming Lyn.

'I think she could do a better job... All right, Evan, I'll see to him.'

Evan turned back, interrupted Ieuan James's conversation with Lyn, made his apologies, shook hands and was gone. Tal smiled at James.

'Well, you won't want to return to Penarth yet. Why not come across to the Red Lion and have a drink? You could do with a gin, couldn't you, Lyn?'

'I could.'

'From what I remember of the Red Lion,' James said, grinning, 'it's not the sort of place a young lady would normally visit.'

'Ah, that presupposes two things. One, that I'm a young lady; two, that things haven't changed.'

'So let's go see,' James suggested.

They installed themselves in the corner of the renovated lounge and Tal brought the drinks across: whisky for himself and James, a gin and tonic for Lyn. James looked around him and commented that the place had certainly changed, though he was none too keen on bright colours and formica-topped tables himself.

'Better than the sawdust and spittoons that I remember here as a young man,' Tal offered.

'Well, at least we know it's now an acceptable haunt for a young lady,' James said, and saluted Lyn with his glass.

'I don't exactly *haunt* the place,' Lyn protested. Tal was amused; she was responding to Ieuan James in a way she did not, normally, to young men. He doubted that she was aware of the effect he was having on her, but her eyes were brighter and a smile came more readily to her lips than was usually the case in company. Normally, she had little time for small talk, and no patience for banter. But this evening she seemed to be enjoying herself.

Ieuan James was more difficult to pinpoint. He *seemed* to be enjoying himself but Tal felt it was all on the surface. There was an inner tension in the man that suggested he had other things on his mind, and while he could chat happily enough with Lyn it was the casual conversation that demanded no intellectual effort; Tal gained the impression that he was carrying out a function that had become almost mechanical, the role of the pleasant party-giver and socialite, *bon viveur* and good companion. It was a role that served to hide the real man underneath.

'Did you ever stay in Pen-Rhys House before?' Tal asked.

'Evan's house?' Ieuan shook his head. 'No; Evan stayed with us – you'll recall no doubt that he was my brother-in-law at one time – a few times in the old days, and he invited me to come up to see the house his father had left him but the chance never came. It's a bit of a Victorian monstrosity, isn't it? But Evan is comfortable enough there.'

'What did you think of his speech to-night?' Lyn asked.

Ieuan nodded thoughtfully as he considered the question. He brushed his long fair hair back from his eyes, took a sip of his whisky and nodded again. 'It was pretty good. He was telling me last night that he has political ambitions, and I explained I could probably introduce him to a few useful people. I think he speaks well enough to forget one hurdle, anyway – his control is better than many politicians I know. He should do well, in my opinion.'

'He strayed a bit from his brief tonight,' Tal suggested.

Ieuan James fixed him with a cool stare that was somehow astir in its depths with a steady calculation. They were the eyes of a hard businessman suddenly. 'How do you mean?'

'He got ... aggressive.'

'I don't follow.'

'I understand what Tal means,' Lyn broke in. 'That bit about the committee membership, and planning decisions and all that. He hasn't come forward with that tack before. In fact, it's not something we've even discussed. It took us both by surprise, as it probably did the rest of the action committee.'

Ieuan finished his drink and stood up. 'That may have been my doing,' he said, and walked away to the bar. He came back a few minutes later with three doubles, and set them down on the table, glanced around the room and nodded. 'Yes, it may have been my doing.'

'I don't understand,' Tal said. 'You've surely come fresh to the whole issue.'

'I'd better explain.' Ieuan James seemed ill at ease, as though conscious that he had stepped into something that was none of his business. He played with his glass between his hands as though thinking hard, trying to find the right words, yet Tal had felt he was a man to whom the right words always came easily.

'It's really the result, I suspect, of a chat we had last night over a meal.'

'You talked about the Hospital Action Committee?'

'Well, when Evan rang me and suggested I should stop over for the meeting this evening after my visit to see the council, I was interested, of course. He gave me some background over the phone; I then put my secretary on to a few people and made a few inquiries. It was that which we talked about last night.'

Tal leaned back and folded his arms. He stared hard at Ieuan James. 'Evan was dropping hints. You gave those hints to him?'

Ieuan James put on his embarrassed look, cocked his head on one side and with a show of reluctance, explained. 'I told you I made inquiries. I came up with nothing positive in the short time available, but I did come up with a few interesting bits of gossip. I should add, hastily, that that's all they are at the moment – gossip. I retailed them to Evan, but I had no idea he was going to be rather … indiscreet, and produce them like a rabbit out of a hat this evening. Not that there's any damage done, I mean no names were mentioned.'

'The reporter from the *Leader* was keen to get it all down,' Tal said grimly.

'That's not necessarily a bad thing,' James commented. 'It could be a useful piece of publicity.'

'I don't think it's the kind of publicity we need.'

'Why not?' James asked in surprise.

'Because it smacks of muck-raking. And we don't know if there's any muck to get raked over.'

'But what if there *is* muck?'

Tal was silent for a moment. He glanced at Lyn; she was staring at Ieuan James, but there was a calculation in her glance that suggested to Tal that she had shed the schoolgirlishness of a few minutes ago. Now she was herself again, and summing up Ieuan James in the manner Tal would have expected of her.

'At the moment,' she said softly, 'all we know is that Evan has publicly stated that certain questions should be asked.

James nodded. 'That's more or less what I said to him. It's true I went a *little* further, but not specifically. I simply pointed out that my ... sources had suggested that there might have been a certain amount of shenanigans going on behind the scenes, and before the

Hospital Action Committee accepts the defeat that may well be on the cards, it ought to put some pressure on certain people.'

'Such as?'

James hesitated, then shrugged. 'Maldwyn Powers?'

Tal took a deep breath. He had known Mal Powers for thirty years. Chairman of the Co-operative Society, a justice of the peace, a headmaster at a local school and a councillor for the last fifteen years, he had come to the valley from Merthyr, where he had made strong political connections, and he had been snapped up into local politics here. He was a hard, tough fighter. He was a man a cause needed on its side. He was outspoken, direct, and made many enemies, but the way he made enemies won him many friends. There were people who disliked him intensely yet voted for him. He was not a man whose company Tal would seek socially; on the other hand, he was not a man Tal had ever heard a word of scandal about.

'He's a Methodist lay preacher with a back and a conscience like a ramrod,' Tal said. 'You're suggesting he's been mixed up in some form of chicanery?'

Ieuan James stared at his drink for a long moment, then shrugged. 'You sound as

84

though you're convinced everything is above board already, so what's the point of my saying anything more?'

'You've given me a name,' Tal said quietly. 'I think you should give me some facts.'

Ieuan James shook his head and smiled. 'I can't do that. Because I haven't got any facts. I told you at the beginning – I've merely heard some rumours. Whether they can be substantiated I don't know. I simply retailed some of the gossip to Evan because he said it could be important. He'll be looking into it, he says. And the name is Maldwyn Powers.'

'Who happens to be the chief antagonist as far as we are concerned. He's right behind the road project, and he has a powerful voice on the council and the planning committee.' Tal grimaced. 'I wouldn't believe he's been tied up in anything shady… But why did you raise this with Evan, anyway?'

Ieuan James sat upright in his chair. He spread his hands wide in a gesture of submission he did not feel. 'Now wait a minute. I didn't raise it with Evan. He talked around the matter, said he needed something to support the fight, and I came up with the rumours. All right, you're critical, but let's get one thing clear. I've no axe to grind – other than the same environmental one you're

sharpening. As far as I'm concerned professionally, it matters not a jot whether the
hospital gets built at Llandarog or Timbuktu.
My tender has been accepted; I'll be doing
the designs. So I'm okay. But like you, and
Lyn here, and like Evan too, I'm concerned
about Llandarog. *That's* my interest. If I've
raised the sort of pressure suggestion you
don't like, I'm sorry. Maybe you think it's …
dirty? There's a lot of dirt in politics. Inevit-
ably, some of it stains the water around here.
Believe me.'

Tal sighed. He had the feeling he was being
unreasonable. He smiled at Ieuan James,
half-apologetically. Rumours were always
about; sometimes they exposed villainy. It
was just that Mal Powers… 'If you'd said it
about Tommy Elias, now, maybe I'd have
taken it better,' he said, almost to himself.

'Pardon?'

'The Trust cottages in Cwmdare,' Lyn explained, thankful to escape what was becoming an awkward subject. 'They are threatened
by a sliding tip, one that Mr Elias has been
tearing into with water jets. The Trust want to
reach a financial agreement, but Elias won't
even meet them. I tell you, it's all environmental problems around here. A legacy of
the past, I suppose.' She hesitated, thought-

fully, then frowned. 'But you'll know Elias, won't you?'

Ieuan James shook his head. 'Don't think so.'

'Surely … didn't you appear on the same television programme with him a little while back? In the Cardiff studios. What was it called … *Confrontation,* wasn't it?'

Ieuan James turned his handsome head to look at her and his eyes widened as he thought back. 'Oh, *that* man Elias! Oh God, yes … I don't *know* him, but I've met him sure enough. You remember that programme? We almost ended up at each other's throats.'

'I recall it got a bit … warm,' Lyn said, smiling.

'Hell, yes.' James grinned at them both. 'Funny, that. I mean, the valley is traditionally regarded as the sort of place where everyone knows everyone else, where we all live in each other's pockets, where you can't spit without the neighbours knowing where you've hawked. I can point to you, Dr Rees, as an instance. Do you remember me coming to your surgery, after a rugby match for the school? You weren't my doctor, but you were the nearest to the pitch. So we've met before, even though I've not lived in the valley for years. Elias, now; he's a few years older than me, I think, but we're roughly contemporary. Both of us from the valley; both of us working from offices in Cardiff. But we've never met until we sit face to face in a Cardiff studio. But damn, a *confrontation* it was! I've never met such an opinionated, stuck-up, self-indulgent animal in my life!'

'It made good television, though,' Lyn said wickedly.

'For you, not for me,' James said with a rueful grin. 'It was architecture versus utility and he really tore into my creative, artistic guts. I almost ended up thumping him. You're right, Dr Rees – if I could have got something on *him* now, over your other local problem, I'd really have worked on it, with pleasure!'

'I think I might even have accepted it, as a gift,' Tal said, and took a stiff drink of whisky.

2

Tal Rees liked the kind of music that raced his blood – Wagner, Khachaturian, the coursing of wild whirling excitement in his veins. He enjoyed sentimental films that brought tears to his eyes and he liked the Welsh

National Stadium on international day, when the teams came out and the deep masculine roar began, rising up like an impassioned hymn that lifted a man, raised him into the sky, made him feel like a god watching and participating in the activities of gods on the field. He could step outside his door late on a frosty night, perhaps on his way to a night call, and the coldness would drive an exhilaration into his chest that gave him a sudden urge to shout aloud, to run, to speed through the darkness, faster than any human being had ever run. It was part of his make-up, a childish inability to control emotion, a revelling in excitement, an indulgence in *feeling*, and this was one of those nights.

They had left Ieuan James, purring away in his big car. He and Lyn had decided they would not go straight back to their respective homes, but would take a walk in the cooling darkness and now they strolled, arms linked, along the road that looped along the side of the mountain. The hills stood around them silently in the darkness, looming large and black, but their outlines were too soft to be menacing, and the lights twinkled up and down the length of the valley like a thousand flares processing endlessly, silently, as they had done for a hundred years. Tal's chest was tight as they walked below the track that led up to Llandarog and he had that old feeling, the one where he wanted to shout aloud in an unreasoning exultation. Perhaps it was the night; perhaps it was the whisky; perhaps it was something else, a name he would not admit to his heart.

'An attractive man,' he said, as they paused to lean on the wooden gate and look down the hill, past the brook that tumbled crazily down through the small clump of pine trees that had been the forerunner of the afforestation scheme now well advanced at the head of the valley.

'Who?'

Tal grinned at her in the darkness. 'Ieuan James.'

'Some would say so.'

'The way you were lapping up his conversation *you* would say so,' he teased her. 'You got almost girlish, Lyn–'

'And that's not like me?' she asked quickly. There was a sudden edge to her tone that stripped away some of the softness of their relationship. 'People react to their companions, Tal.'

He nodded in submission. 'I'm no conversationalist, no social animal like Ieuan James.'

'But you're a *real* person.'

'Meaning he's not?' Tal asked, interested that she should have detected the same superficiality as he had done.

'I don't think he's real,' Lyn said, 'not in his personal relationships – as far as we are concerned, anyway. True, we're virtual strangers to him, but ... well, you say I reacted to him, and I did, because there was no danger in it, do you know? It was all on a level that meant nothing. Whatever we said to each other would be forgotten as soon as we parted; like putting whitewash on a wall in a rainstorm, once on, it's gone. That's how it is with Ieuan James, I felt. He talked, chatted, flirted–'

'Oh yes!'

'Flirted,' she repeated firmly, and squeezed his arm, 'but it was all a front, ephemeral, meaning nothing. Maybe that's how his marriage broke up... I mean, it's possible there's no give in the man, no depth, perhaps he's not capable of creating a true relationship with a woman... He's charming, mind,' she added, almost as an afterthought.

'An attractive man, as I said.'

'Well ... I suppose so. But I say it reluctantly. With an unsophisticated woman he could score heavily, I suppose.'

'But not with you.'

'I'm sophisticated. Thirty, anyway.'

'And not married,' Tal said involuntarily. Since the words were out, and a small silence followed, he hurried on, 'I've wondered about that, Lyn. You've had chances.'

'I have,' she said soberly.

'That librarian fellow–'

'Fred Thomas. He was really only interested in Hannibal. No other passion could take his place.'

'You're laughing at me. I'm serious! I don't understand how an attractive, intelligent girl like you – I mean, I thought from the way Evan Ritchie looked at you occasionally he might be working up an interest...'

'He was.' Lyn tugged at Tal's arm and they turned away from the gate, began to retrace their steps along the road and back towards the village. 'But I suppose you could say he has a lesbian relationship with me.'

'A what?'

Lyn began to giggle. 'Your classical education is wanting, Tal. Catullus ... *Odi et amo* ... I hate and I love? Catullus and Lesbia: Evan Ritchie is a bit like that with me. There's been a sort of undeclared sex war between us ever since he caught me in the surgery about eighteen months ago. I think he was feeling a bit excitable that night, and he got a bit … forward, shall I say? It was like he was possessed of the old Adam. I could have let him down lightly, but he was a bit too insistent for my maidenly modesty to accept, so I tripped him verbally, flattened his ego, ripped away his figurative oak leaf and dusted him down with itching powder. So now he's a mass of unresolved urges and neuroses. He'd like to get me to bed and hates me for making him feel lustful.' She paused. 'There might even be a bit of the *odi* thing in his reaction to the abortion matter with Willy Thatch's wife.'

Tal was silent for a moment as they paced slowly down the hill. He looked down to the pools of light in the streets below them; cars flashed through the darkened roadways but up here all was a clinging darkness.

'You were still wrong and Evan was right. I have to say that, Lyn. You should have consulted us.'

'I know it.'

'And what are we to do now?' Tal asked.

Her grip on his arm slackened slightly and her answer was slow in coming. 'Do you have a choice?' she asked.

'I suppose it depends in part upon Evan–'

'No. I think it depends on me. Evan has made his point, and in a way he's right. I deliberately avoided consulting him. So ethically I'm in the wrong. And there has to be trust between partners.'

'I wouldn't want you to do anything rash, Lyn.'

'I know that.'

They said no more, but walked slowly on, enjoying the night, except for Tal most of the enjoyment and all of the exultation had gone. The night remained the same, the air soft and balmy, a cool summer night like the ones he could remember as a young man when he had come courting on these hills, before university had beckoned. The hills were the same, the rushing sounds from the valley floor, cars and people and life spreading through the streets, it was all the same. But he was different, his mood had changed. The old sadnesses were creeping back into his veins; nothing to do with Lyn, really, but to do with the past, and the years that had slipped away, and the regrets.

It was at moments like these that he could look around him and see himself as part of a close-locked community, secure and safe and happy, and yet at the same time he could look up and see the peaks of his profession, like distant mountains tipped with glittering snowcaps, sunlit and bright, beckoning to a man who once aspired to reach them but who now saw them too distant and too dear in human terms. The years had gone and opportunities had been lost, but the regrets were real enough. Except that when morning came the regrets were gone too as he faced the round and met the people who were part of his life – and he of theirs.

But it could have been different. It would have been different, but for one searing moment of carelessness.

He walked silently down the mountain road with Lyn, and neither of them spoke until they came to the bungalow set back from the road in its own small garden, and she asked him if he'd like to come in for a nightcap before he made his way back to his own house and the surgery.

'I ought to go back, in case there've been calls,' he said doubtfully.

'Evan's duty night, after the meeting. And there's the phone, after all.'

He went in with her. She offered whisky, coffee or chocolate. He chose hot chocolate but she gave him a brandy in addition, knowing his predilections. She knew him very well.

They finished their drinks and sat in silence watching an old film on television. It was a companionable feeling, seated in her living-room, watching television, and yet it left him with a sense of unease too. It was as though he should be here with someone else, as ghosts hovered behind his shoulder as they had done for fifteen years and more. But when the film ended Lyn switched the set off, and they sat on in the semi-darkness, the room lit only by the single standard lamp in the corner. At last, almost dreamily, Lyn spoke.

'I suppose I could start a practice in Cardiff.'

'What's wrong with a practice here in the valley?'

'And compete with you?' She snorted. 'Wouldn't stand a chance.'

'The valley needs good medics, and it's not a competition, anyway.'

'It's not the point,' she said in a voice that was suddenly tired. 'It's time I left the partnership. I've stayed too long. For the wrong reasons.'

The words hung there in the air and he told himself he should not ask for an explanation – it was too dangerous, too problematical – but the question came out in spite of himself.

'What do you mean, wrong reasons?'

She did not answer immediately, but she did not look at him either. Her chin sank to her chest, and it was almost as though she felt a certain humiliation. Perhaps she did, and he agonized silently for her.

'I *should* have come back to the valley after university because I wanted to serve the community that reared me.' Her voice grew softer. 'It should have been because I was imbued with a sense of mission and purpose, a desire to heal people I loved and wanted to be among.'

'I advised you against coming back. You could have gone to one of the big teaching hospitals in London. You could have become–'

'I could have done all sorts of things, as *you* could have, Tal. You advised me to break away. But like you I didn't. You had the brains and the drive and the opportunity to reach the heights of the profession, but you didn't – for the wrong reasons. And I fell into the same trap.'

'I didn't–'

Lyn shook her head. 'Not trap; that's the wrong word. Too emotive; it was of my own making, after all. No, it was just that I knew what I wanted, that's all.'

He had known what he had wanted too, when he was a young man. At twenty-five the whole of the medical world had beckoned to him, he had married a woman he loved very much, and then there had been the rending, screaming metal, the car twisting and leaping like a crazed salmon in the darkness, and his life had changed. He wanted only security; he desired burial; he wanted the arms of a mother around him to comfort him and the valley had been his mother. Work had been the palliative; involvement the cure; people the antidote to thought and pain. Until it was too late for ambition, too far to go back, too deeply enmeshed to escape. Even if he had wanted to escape. But Lyn–

It was as though she had read his thoughts.

'I saw you that summer,' she said, 'after your wife died. I saw the way you immersed yourself in the valley. And the picture was still with me when I came out to practise years later. I came back to the valley and worked here – against your advice – for reasons that were so simple yet so complex too. I wanted to work here because *you* worked here. I wanted to be in the valley because *you* lived here. And the summit of *my* ambition was to work with you. It still is, Tal.'

He shook his head. 'Don't say any more, Lyn.'

'I've started. Let me finish. I came back wanting to give you something you'd lost, and I thought that one day you'd see it in my eyes. But you never did. Or if you did, you ignored it.'

'I saw an infatuation in a young woman's eyes,' Tal said sadly. 'I couldn't presume on that.'

'I'm older now,' she said.

'And I'm too old.'

'I will always deny that, Tal.'

She was looking at him directly but he could not speak. It was not that he did not want to; it was simply that he could not find the right words. There were unspoken things between them, the problem of memories and loyalties, and inside him too the spectre of failure. The valley had meant security once, when his world had collapsed; it could collapse about him completely if he was wrong about his feelings for Lyn. He dared not expose them, not even after all these years, for he was too much of a coward. There was the chance that if he did, he would not measure up to the image she had of him.

What was it that old woman from Caergwent had said to him when he was a student? She had spoken of images, and she had shattered him with her words. Facing Lyn now, the words were not easy. What could he say to her?

In a moment, as the syllables trembled on his lips, his dilemma was resolved.

The telephone rang.

3

Tal rose and looked around him.

The Patch looked quite different under present circumstances. It was just a piece of waste ground really, no different from many in the valley. Years ago it had been used as a siding when the trucks had pulled in on the small colliery branch line to be loaded. But the pit had been closed for over forty years and the railway lines had long since vanished. The Patch had stayed on as an open space, flanked on three sides by the backs of terrace houses, mean, narrow and dilapidated, a group of streets through which policemen in the Depression had walked only in pairs. The fourth side of the square was matted with bulrushes, the swampy area that faced the river as it meandered sluggishly down along the valley floor.

The Patch was not always a dreary place. Once a year, in late November, a family of doubtful origins visited the Patch, bringing with them seven Dodgem Cars, five sideshows at six new pence a throw, a Noah's Ark and a blaring organ that sent a cacophony of popular music echoing against the backs of the resilient houses. Years ago, Tal remembered, they had also brought with them a portable loo at the council's insistence, but in the end they hadn't bothered any more; it wasn't necessary, with the river there. But on the occasions when the fair arrived there had been a blaze of colour on the Patch: the paint of the Noah's Ark was faded and dated, but it gleamed well enough under the bright coloured lights, and though the bunting and streamers that hung from the sideshows were somewhat tattered and threadbare, they danced under the breeze and the music and the screaming of young girls unimpressed by the rickety Dodgems and prancing dragons but anxious to draw attention to themselves.

Tonight, the Patch was neither dreary nor colourful. At the entrance to the Patch from Madelaine Street a knot of women stood, shawls over their shoulders, arms folded, the older ones with curlers in their hair, the younger ones shrouded in headscarves. At the far entrance to the Patch – near Coram Street – there was a group of men, who had spilled out of the Duke of Monmouth when the news had first broken half an hour since. Keeping both groups at bay were five helmeted policemen – two local men, and three others drafted in from higher up the valley. And on the inside was Tal, Inspector Jack Arthur, and a couple of young constables who seemed to be all eyes and open mouths. Over them all played an eerie blue light, the reflection from the police ambulance, the squad cars, and the hospital ambulance. The vehicles blazed headlights on the small group in the centre, near the hastily erected canvas screen, but the whiteness of this light seemed in no way to remove the blue-washed effect, and the faces around Tal seemed strange and unfamiliar.

He looked around him as though seeking a point of reference, something on which he could seize to return to reality, but the reality lay at his feet.

She lay in a twisted heap with her head at an unnatural angle, her dark hair fluffed up untidily, her dead face gleaming with an almost phosphorescent glow in the blazing headlights of the cars. Her hands were spread wide, fingers crooked, digging into the dirt, and her legs seemed to be braced as though she had arched her back in a last struggle for breath against the hands that had killed her.

Her skirt had ridden up over her thighs and her underclothes had been torn away; her legs were long and slim, her shoes still on her feet, incongruous in view of the violence of her death. She wore a pale green short jacket and it too had been torn at the shoulder, as though a predatory hand had grasped at her, dragged her down for the assault. There were traces of dirt down the front of her skirt and along the sleeve of her jacket as though she had rolled, fighting in the darkness.

Jack Arthur stood at Tal's elbow looking down at the girl. He was built like a wardrobe: dark, square, solid, immovable, with the kind of shoulders that suggested he had spent his formative years swinging a pick at the coalface. He was held in some awe and considerable respect in the valley: a local man who had worked in the Metropolitan Police for thirteen years before returning home, he was known to have a quick mind, a sharp temper, and a deep sympathy for people who deserved it. He obviously felt that the person who had killed the girl at his feet deserved no sympathy at all.

'Strangulation?' he asked.

Tal nodded. 'Looks like it. But we'll have to do a postmortem, of course.'

'You finished?'

'Yes. All I can do by way of preliminary work. When will Tom Spinney be able to take over?'

'The summer influenza which has struck down our revered police surgeon could well be finished by the weekend,' Arthur said coldly. 'By which time most of the difficult work will have been done. I'm grateful, anyway, Dr Rees, that you were able to come.'

'Yes.' Tal eyed the corpse at his feet in gloomy silence. Arthur waved to the small knot of men standing at the edge of the circle and the man with the dangling cameras came forward. The same man who had been present as representative for the *Leader* at the Hospital Action Committee meeting tried to join him, but a growl from Jack Arthur sent him scurrying back out of range. Arthur directed the cameraman to finish the work he had started before Tal arrived and then spoke to the ambulance regarding the arrangements for transporting the body in the shell to the mortuary in Pontypridd. He turned back to Tal, who was still staring moodily at the body.

'You recognize her?'

'Aye.' He nodded slowly and sadly. 'She came to see me. She's called Barbara – Barbara Porelli.'

The tea in the police canteen was of a strange consistency and taste, but at this time of night anything that was hot and liquid was welcome. There was the taste of dust and death in Tal's throat, not the kind of death he was used to, a quiet slipping away in the dusk of life, but a violent twisting, hammering of frantic heels on a dirty ground, a bitten lip, a young woman going before her time, long before her time. Tal had seen such death before in the hospitals – victims of car accidents, factory injuries, bad falls, but never murder. This kind of death was new to him and his stomach was stiff, the muscles contorted into a twisted, numb state that made him feel that he wanted the reality of hot liquid to bring it back to a lifelike state. He sat alone in the canteen, waiting for Jack Arthur as he said he would.

There were three other duty constables in the room; they kept apart from him even though they knew him. Perhaps they realized he was waiting for the inspector.

Jack Arthur came in some ten minutes later, as Tal was starting another cup of tea. Arthur obtained one for himself, sat down beside Tal and stirred some sugar into his tea with angry jerks of his wrist.

'Bloody reporters. Make me sick. Got enough to do without havin' to make statements, haven't I?'

'They've got a job.'

'Suppose. But what a bloody job, isn't it?' He sipped his tea and wrinkled his nose, stirred in another spoonful of sugar. 'Hate this stuff, I do, but you need a cup of tea this time in the morning. Now then, Barbara Porelli, you said.'

'That's right.' Tal nodded. 'You'll remember her father. Sold up the café in Lloyd Street and opened the icecream parlour – you know, swish place – in Edwardstown. It was his wife who ran it – he was a bit of a billiards king. Still is, while he can manoeuvre his belly over the baize.'

'She's not living in the valley now,' Arthur said, frowning. 'We found her handbag, you know, and the address she got there is a Cardiff address. Flat, looks like. We're getting it checked out now.'

'That's right. She left the valley when she was seventeen, eighteen, I suppose. Took some job in Cardiff or wherever...' Tal hesitated, inhibited by the traditional ingrained medical prejudice against disclosing details of the personal lives of patients. But this was different. 'I think she went a bit wild after leaving home – probably before leaving home, too. Welsh-Italian parentage can be a funny mixture, you know, and some of the restrictions must have been too much for Barbara. There were more than a few boys in the valley, and after she went to Cardiff there were more than a few men.'

'Names?'

When Tal made no reply, Jack Arthur shook his head. He ridged his brows in thought and glared at his tea. 'No good keeping quiet, Dr Rees. Murder, this is. All information will have to be checked. And any names you got about her Cardiff escapades, we got to have. Check them, then. Never know what'll turn up in routine checks, you see.'

'I haven't got names,' Tal replied. 'The fact is she came to me some time back – I'd have to look in my files for precise details – and she had a miscarriage. Then she was back a bit later, and this time we had to arrange an abortion. After that–'

'Cardiff bicycle, is it? Anybody could have a ride,' Arthur sneered.

Tal was silent for a moment. Then he shook his head slowly. 'No. Not quite like that. I didn't see her as … as the kind of whore you suggest. She kicked over the traces, shrugged off parental control, went a bit wild like you said, but it was a sort of ... *experimentation*, I think. Experimentation, and, well, perhaps a challenge too. For herself, and to those people who knew her. She was sort of telling everybody that it was her body and her life and she could use both the way she wanted.'

'So–'

'Wait a minute. All right, there are plenty of girls like that in Bute Street, and some of them end up in diseased back alleys. But I never thought Barbara would end up like that. To start with, she was an intelligent girl. Second, she had an independence of mind that would eventually have made her get on to straight rails – rails of her choosing, mind, but straight, *committed* rails. And it might be that she had already found those rails.'

'How do you mean?'

'She came to see me this week. She was pregnant again.'

Arthur raised his eyebrows as though Tal's statement answered all sorts of questions. For Tal, it answered none, but simply posed more.

'Don't jump to conclusions,' he said. 'She came to me pregnant, and I thought immediately she wanted me to arrange another abortion. I even started to suggest that she should think about her responsibilities – but the fact is, she didn't ask for an abortion. All she asked for was confirmation of pregnancy. I confirmed it, and went for her, you know, got all moral, like. I think that's maybe what she wanted.'

'A lecture?' Arthur asked in surprise. 'She came to you to be told off, not to have an abortion?'

'I don't know. Maybe. Fact is, I asked why did she come back to me, here in the valley, at all, when she could have gone to someone in Cardiff where they didn't know her background, and it would have been almost anonymous. I think the answer is that she came back because she was changing – or maybe, *reverting* is the right word.'

'You've lost me.'

Tal pursed his lips, scratched his cheek thoughtfully and glowered. He shook his head, as though trying to jumble his thoughts, give them time and opportunity to fall into a new pattern, from which he could construct a logically argued shape. 'Let me put it like this. Barbara Porelli went to Cardiff and lived the life of a hedonist, as far as she could afford. But when trouble hit her she came back to the valley – twice. To me. Why? Because whether she liked it or not, her true values – the ones that had been

109

inculcated into her – lay here in the valley. The odd thing, of course, is that some of them were her parents' values and you can hardly say that they were valley *mores*, but let that pass. Maybe South Italy and Merthyr Tydfil are not that far apart in some ways, where social customs are concerned. So I think she came back here for medical solutions to her problems when what she was really seeking, inside, were moral values.'

'Far-fetched.'

'Could be. And no real evidence to support it. Except–'

'Except what?'

'This last visit.' Tal picked up Arthur's spoon, began to toy with it absent-mindedly. 'I got the impression something had happened.'

'She was pregnant again.'

'No, not just that. Her pregnancy meant something different to her. She had reached a decision, I think, before she ever came to my surgery. But she wanted me to rant at her, so she'd be confirmed in her decision. She *wanted* me to shout at her about responsibilities. She had already decided to keep the baby when it was born–'

'And marry the father?'

'Well, that's it. I don't know. She was a bit

tight-lipped. She had decided to do *some-thing*. And she said something ... odd.'

'Like what?' Arthur asked gruffly, some-what uneasy at Tal's analysing of Barbara Porelli's actions. He liked facts, not theories about what went on inside a person's mind.

'She said she was going to ... sort it out. She said ... or at least she left me with the impression that she was going to face up to the father of the child she was carrying and put the facts to him.'

'Get him to marry her?'

'She didn't say that. Rather ... she said she needed to get some money. And that the man ... had some money behind him.'

'Aaaah.' Jack Arthur let out a long pent-up sigh, laden with wisdom and understanding. 'Now you're talking a bit of sense, Dr Rees. I'm beginning to get the picture. She chases around, gets up the stick, decides to put the screws on the man who did the dirty deed. She wants to bring up the kid, but inde-pendent-like, she'll do it on her own. As long as he coughs up the cash to support her. Marriage, she isn't interested in. Why? Maybe because it's not *on*.'

'How do you mean?' Tal asked, baffled in his turn.

'Because the chap's married already,'

Arthur said blandly. 'She's carrying his kid, she wants money because she knows she can't get him to marry her. She approaches him, he gets stroppy, she threatens him, so he strangles her. That's it.'

'What's it?'

'A lead. And a bloody good one. If we can now find a man to fit the description we're quids in.'

'What description?'

'A man who had it away recently with Barbara Porelli. A married man. A man with a bit of cash behind him. A man from the valley. With all that, if we can tie him in with a time and a bit of circumstantial evidence, we're clear. It's–'

'Too simple.'

'Maybe,' Arthur said heavily, and began to rise. 'But you come up with something better, tied to *facts*, and I'll go along with it. Meanwhile, I'd better get on, looking for the married valley man who preferred knocking her off to paying her off.'

'And the sexual assault?'

Arthur glowered at Tal Rees. 'Not proved yet. Besides, maybe he decided to have one last nibble at the biscuit. I'll see you, Dr Rees – and thanks for your help. Statement and a look at your files later.'

Willy Thatch's wife was a small woman with lined cheeks and eyes that still smiled. She was quiet, even mouse-like, and yet there was a certain inner warmth about her that gave her an attraction many people were drawn to, even if they did not recognize it. Possibly, it was simply that she was a good listener. Or it might have been that coming from a large family herself, having a large family, and bearing the misfortune of loving a man like Willy Thatch had given her a rare quality.

She certainly did love her husband, for all his weaknesses and his faults. Tal was sure of it. Her eyes clouded sometimes when she spoke of him and she never mentioned his worthlessness. He was her man and there was no gainsaying it.

Tal had thought it necessary to call at the hospital in Church Village where she was being prepared for the abortion. Strictly speaking, she was Lyn's patient, not his, but Tal knew that Lyn would have no objections to his visit. It was all part of his way of doing things: he knew the people of the valley intimately as friends, as well as patients, and his visit to Mrs Jones he knew was in a dual capacity: he came as a doctor to whisper words of encouragement, and as a friend to see that she was comfortable and relaxed.

'One worry I got, Dr Rees,' Mrs Jones said, and the cloudy look was in her eyes.

'The children?'

She shook her head, and allowed a wry smile to touch her faded mouth. 'Oh no ... my eldest, she's a good girl and she can get the breakfast and see the others off to school and all that, and even look after the baby too. No ... it's Willy I'm worried about.'

'It's he who should be worrying about you,' Tal said gently. 'Has he been down to see you?'

'Ah, it's a long trip down, you know, Dr Rees, and the buses aren't frequent, are they? And he's got the allotment to look after, you know.'

Tal had seen it: a wild jungle of grass and fern and wild-thriving lupins, blue and white, the despair of other allotment holders and subject of letters from the council – 'Work it or else'. But it was an excuse that Mrs Jones was happy enough to seize upon as a reason for Willy Thatch's absences at the Alexandra Hotel.

'But you've been in here for four days,' Tal

said. 'I'd have thought he would have come down to see you before now.'

'Well, we didn't expect it to be this long, did we? Wouldn't have been, but for that surgeon wanting some blood checks carried out or something … got funny blood, I have, or so they tell me. Shortage of it there is, so they won't operate until they get the right stuff to put in me, if they need to. Or somethin' like that, anyway. Don't understand it really. Anyway, I'm glad you came, Doctor, because I wanted to ask if you'd pop in and see how Willy is.' She hesitated, conscious that the demands on a doctor's time were numerous, and her anxiety about her husband would need form and substance to justify Tal's visiting him. 'Had a bit of a cold on his chest, he has, this last week. Don't want him to be stuck in bed, you know.'

Tal smiled, nodded, squeezed her hand. 'I'll get over to the house to see how he – and the family – are getting on. But I think you'll be out in a few days anyway and as long as you rest for a while after getting home you'll be all right.'

Except that there would be no rest for her. Willy Thatch was a demanding husband whose sexual appetites were strong, and he would not want to be denied for long with his wife at home. It would now be some weeks since he had had sexual relations with his wife anyway; when she had first visited Lyn at the surgery, it had been because anxiety over her pregnancy had had physical and emotional effects that had made her keep Willy Thatch from her. Tal had not had the full story, but he understood from Lyn that Mrs Jones had been close to a nervous breakdown, brought on by her own inhibitions, her almost religious conviction that she should give Willy Thatch what he wanted when he wanted it, and by the terror of a continuing physical relationship whose demands could well be killing her. For a small, mousy, likeable, brave woman, she was a complex person who could be difficult – and yet so easy – to understand. But that was what people were all about, Tal thought to himself; they were immensely complex groupings of nerve-ends and cells, reaching for stars and fumbling in muck.

And he would never understand them, as he would never understand himself.

He went the rounds of the wards in the hospital, chatting to some of the nurses, having a cup of coffee with matron, visiting some of the valley people he had arranged to be sent to the hospital. All seemed glad to see him, except Mrs O'Hara who kept her earphones firmly clamped on her head and refused to speak to him, but she was perhaps most pleased of all that he had come. It was three in the afternoon before he went back out to his car.

The hospital was perched on the top of a small hillock a few miles from Pontypridd, and it gave a sweeping view of the near countryside with its green fields and lurching mountains leading up into the valley. Southwards he could see scattered farms, the first of the rich vale that ran down to the sea. He stood for a few minutes in the car park, listening to a thrush in the rhododendrons to his right, and looking out over the hills; he was thinking about a time when he had come here, years ago, shattered emotionally, wanting to die, as his wife had died, and yet conscious too that death was not the answer – the security of the valley, the need to be loved and used, these were the salvation for him. His mind was a long way distant, latched to memory, when the voice came at his back.

'Dr Rees?'

Tal snapped his thoughts back to the present, turned, and saw the young man standing just behind him. He was perhaps twenty-five years old, slimly built, with the loose ranginess of a young colt. His face was thin and tanned, his eyes an intense bright blue, and his hair was worn long, very straight, its straw colour framing his face and heightening the sharpness of his eyes. He was a little above middle height, and he wore plum-coloured jeans that fitted tightly over narrow hips, and a pale yellow patterned shirt that showed the leanness of his chest, the flatness of his stomach. He had the look of a sprinter, Tal thought, with all the tension of the starting blocks. But what was the reason for tension?

'I'm Colin Owen,' the young man said.

Tal put out an unrecognising hand. 'Hello,' he said.

A flicker of annoyance touched the young man's mouth as he took Tal's hand and shook it; it was as though he expected to be known by his name, and was angry that the knowledge was not there.

'Cyfarthfa Owen's son,' he said, not liking the words.

'Ah,' Tal said non-commitally, but he knew about the young man now. Cyfarthfa Owen was an unusual man. He lived at the head of the valley and was a teacher in a primary school – senior master. He was something of a poet, having entered pieces at the National Eisteddfod though never winning a prize. His greatest claim to fame was the fact that he had played for Wales eighteen times as a wing three-quarter and had programmes to prove it. But his oddity was that his grandfather had owned a bus company and left a great deal of money to Cyfarthfa – who in turn had set up a trust fund for his only son, Colin. Cyfarthfa could afford to live and work in the valley, happily, comfortably, and never worry about inflation and prices, because there was all that money locked away and his own little fame among his people. For Colin, it was different. He wasn't Colin Owen, he was Cyfarthfa Owen's son; he had his own worlds to conquer, his own way to make; the need to struggle would never be there with the cushion of a trust fund to soften any fall; an academic career was now almost over, and soon there would be a job, and the real test to come. Tal guessed it would be a traumatic test, from the hints of deep panic in the man's eyes, a restless anxiety that displayed a lack of assurance in his capabilities.

'Did you want to see me about something?' Tal asked.

Colin Owen hesitated. 'I wanted a chat... Perhaps we could walk around the grounds for a few minutes?'

'If you like.'

Tal turned and began to walk up the hill, away from the car park. The thrush threshed away in the rhododendrons at their approach and Colin Owen seemed momentarily startled. Then he bowed his head, locked his hands behind his back and paced at Tal's side, saying nothing.

They passed the hospital block and continued to climb the gentle rise. A slight breeze ruffled at their hair and the grass was springy under their feet as they left the path and walked towards the seats that had been placed at the top of the slope for recuperating inmates of the hospital to enjoy sunshine and clean air. Tal glanced towards the young man at his side; the head was still lowered.

'You still at university?' Tal asked.

Owen licked his lips. 'Finish this year.'

'What will you do then?'

'Got the offer of a job with ICI.'

'It wasn't chemistry you were reading, was it?'

The fair head shook a negative response, and the blue eyes flickered a quick glance at Tal and then away around the hillside. 'No, no. It was physics, in fact, but then I went on to read for an MSc. And now I'm just

120

finishing an MBA – a Master's in Business Administration.'

'So they'll be taking you on as a business whizz-kid, not as a physicist, is it?' Tal asked, smiling.

There was no smile in response. 'That's right. Physicists are two a penny.'

The conversation died. They reached the top of the slope and looked about them. Tal waited, barely conscious of the blue of the sky and the green of the hillside and the whiteness of the hospital walls. There was an internal struggle going on in the young man standing beside him; it ended, as Colin Owen, almost with a gasp, said, 'You were down at the Patch the other night.'

Something happened in Tal's veins. 'That's right.'

'You examined her.'

'Yes.'

There was a short silence. Tal turned slowly, looked straight at Colin Owen. 'Did you know Barbara Porelli?'

'She ... she came to see you.'

'How did you know that?' Tal asked.

'She told me.'

This time he did gasp as he spoke, so that Tal hardly caught the words. But their import was clear enough for him, and his throat was suddenly dry.

'When did she tell you?'

Colin Owen brushed the question aside, like a colt brushing impatiently at an importunate fly. 'What do the police think?' he asked.

'You'd better ask them.'

The statement startled Owen. He flashed a quick glance around the hillside as though seeking escape from a trap, but there was no escape; he could walk away, but what little he had already said seemed to tie him to Tal.

'It was you who got her pregnant,' Tal said grimly, and Colin Owen shivered.

'I wanted her to marry me,' he said in a miserable voice.

'You'd better tell me the whole story,' Tal suggested, knowing Owen wanted just such encouragement.

It was quickly told, once the young man started. He had known Barbara slightly for years. Five or six years ago, he could not quite remember when but before she had left the valley, when she was still at school, there had been some abortive, furtive fumbling in the ferns above Treharne, but he had been inexperienced and she indifferent. They had gone their own ways until perhaps six months ago they had met by chance in

Cardiff. He had been doing some research in a company in Cardiff for his MBA and she had been working in the company. He had invited her out, they had met several times, and at last he had taken her back to his flat where they had slept together one weekend. Thereafter they had met regularly.

'The thing was, she was different from what she used to be,' Owen said, twisting his face at the memory. 'She used to be wild, and she told me about some of the parties, but that was the point, see, she was *telling* me so that there wouldn't be anything unsaid between us, you know? We were suddenly involved in a way she – and I – had never been involved before. I ... I *loved* her.'

'Was she in love with you?' Tal asked.

The grimace became more pronounced as though the memory was scarred. 'She never said so. She used to laugh at me a bit. But the way she behaved ... I think she was in love with me. And I told her ... I wanted to marry her.'

'Was that before or after you learned she was pregnant?'

There was a certain indignation in Owen's glance. 'Before, dammit! I tell you, I asked her to marry me, and she wouldn't give me an answer. And then she phoned me from the valley, and it sort of came out that she'd been to see you, and I eventually got out of her that she was pregnant. And you know what she said then?' The indignation was no longer directed towards Tal, but towards the dead girl. 'She said she didn't want to see me any more!'

Tal frowned. 'I don't understand. After my confirmation she was pregnant she said she wanted to finish with you?'

'That's exactly it. Now what the hell did you say to her? Why did she reach that decision?'

He wanted to blame Tal, and there was the anger of rejection in his eyes. It suddenly came to Tal that Colin Owen may well have been shattered by the news of Barbara Porelli's death, and frightened by his involvement with her and the possible consequences of it, but his major preoccupation was with her rejection of him shortly before she died. It was sufficiently fierce to cause him to cast away discretion.

Quietly, Tal said, 'I told her it was time she stopped going to bed with every man who moved into her sights. I told her she ought to settle down. I asked her whether she'd thought of accepting her responsibilities. I suggested she should seriously consider

124

marrying the father of her child.'

'You said that to her?' Owen's voice was incredulous. 'But she told me on the phone… You must have said something else! Why the hell did she tell me we were finished?'

Tal began to understand. Cyfarthfa Owen's son had been rejected for himself, and needed to know why.

'I think you should have anxieties other than those that seem to be bothering you,' Tal said.

'What do you mean?'

'Barbara is dead.'

'I know that!'

'Murdered.'

'Of course I–' Owen stopped speaking and stared at Tal. Slowly, the blood drained from his face, so that his tan became an unhealthy yellowish tinge on his skin. 'What are you trying to say?'

'A simple enough statement. Barbara Porelli is dead. She was the victim of a sexual assault, it would seem. She was strangled afterwards. The motive is not certain. Some of the contents of her handbag were taken. But the police are pursuing one line of inquiry for sure. They are looking for the man who got Barbara Porelli pregnant. They think he is a married man, with money in the bank – money Barbara wanted to get her hands on, so that she could bring up that child she was carrying.'

'But I asked her to marry me! And I'm not poor, for God's sake!'

'You still don't get the point.'

Puzzlement chased anxiety across Colin Owen's face like shadows on a hillside. At the back of his mind was the danger Tal spoke of, but it was held there by the more frontal problems for him – why had Barbara turned him down? The lurking anxiety nevertheless came thrusting through, slowly, unbidden. It came to the front when Tal spoke.

'I think you should go and talk to the police.'

The alarm in Owen's face was now clear. 'What for? I only came to you to ask you what you'd said to her – why she had phoned me to say... You're a *doctor!*'

'So?'

Owen shook his head in confusion. 'If I spoke to you, there'd be no question of it going further–'

'Professional confidences? You're not my patient, Colin. I'm under no vow of silence.'

'You mean you'll tell the police about me and Barbara?'

'They're looking for you, Colin.'

'No!' he said vehemently. 'They're looking for someone else, the man who killed her. A married man, you said... *Did* she have someone else... Was I really the father of that kid? No, they're not looking for me; hell ... I don't know what's going on, what it's all about...'

'They're looking for Barbara's lover, Colin. That's you.' Tal regarded him dispassionately for a moment as the young man kept his head averted. 'It would be simpler – and more sensible – if you went to the police yourself.'

'You'll tell them, if I don't?'

Tal hesitated, as the blue eyes, suddenly vulnerable, questioned him. He chewed at his lip, found a scale of dry skin, teased it free, nibbled at it thoughtfully. Then he shook his head. 'I don't know. I just think you ought to go to Jack Arthur and come clean.'

'Perhaps...' Colin Owen hesitated, looked around him but saw nothing. 'I don't know. Why the hell did she say that to me? And *was* there someone else? I can't be sure...' He glared at Tal, as though he was the man responsible for all the troubles of Colin Owen. 'I don't know. Perhaps I'll go to tell them... You won't speak until I've decided what to do?'

Tal said nothing, but watched the young man, and was unable to keep the hint of contempt out of his eyes.

'Something…' Colin Owen whispered unhappily, 'something might turn up…'

CHAPTER III

'We got the head and the haunches in the fridge,' Adams the Rag said, wiping his hands delicately on a piece of cheesecloth. 'You want a look?'

Tal shook his head, not trusting himself to speak. He supposed, as a doctor, he ought to have grown the same kind of shell covering that Joe Adams had for emotional skin, but he had never been able to adopt the casual, careless attitude towards death that the pathologist had. Not that there was anything unusual about Joe Adams: there were many forensic scientists like him. It was as though, in time, they came to treat the subjects of their investigations in precisely the same manner – whether they were pieces of timber or flakes of paint, car bodies or corpses. They were objects, and they bore no relation to human beings.

Not that the photographs Tal was studying

bore much relationship to the human being he had known as Barbara Porelli. The corpse had been photographed on the pathologist's slab, and while it bore a vague resemblance to the girl Tal had known, it could just as easily have been a wax model of the living person. It lacked character and vibrancy; it lacked life. Tal could not even feel that the photograph was of her – he could have been looking at a stranger. But people became strangers after death.

Even so, the thought of her dismembered body frozen as evidence...

He glanced at the little man who stood watching him. Adams the Rag had hit the local headlines once, years ago, when he had proved a local councillor had been involved in a shoplifting incident, by demonstrating in court how the fibres from a piece of cloth torn from a jacket matched those in a suit owned by the councillor. 'Adams, the Rag and the Light-Fingered Councillor', had been the headline in the Sunday papers, and Adams the Rag it had been thereafter. He was proud of the sobriquet, as he was proud of his skill. He handled many of the paint-flake cases in Wales and all of the murders; in some areas of pathology he was a leading expert. His own major interest was the dating of skeletal remains, but though he lectured on the subject at the University of Wales he had few opportunities to practise his skill in general.

'Funny business, this,' Adams said reflectively.

'Barbara Porelli?'

'Aye.' Adams peered thoughtfully at Tal. 'I understand she came to you about her pregnancy.'

'That's right.'

'Well, she was pregnant all right. But this sexual assault is a bit odd.' Adams inspected his fingernails, picked away at the cuticle of one finger with sharp little teeth. 'In fact, the assault was a bit ... kinky.'

Tal put the photographs down on the desk in front of him and perched on a high stool beside the bench under the window. He was not sure that he wanted to be told the details of Barbara's death, and yet there was something which had drawn him down to Pontypridd Forensic Laboratories to talk to Joe Adams.

'What have you got on it all?' he asked in a dry, husky voice.

Joe Adams sat down, folded his arms across his narrow chest and watched a young lab assistant cross the yard outside the window.

'Well, it's a funny conglomeration, really. Not at all what the police want, but you know what they are like, Tal: they work out their lovely little theories and then come chasin' after me to provide evidence to fit in with their theories. They don't want to know what I found; they just want me to find what they say.'

'Hard life.'

'Aye… Anyway, first of all, time of death. The girl wasn't dead for long before she was found. The woman who came out of the pub – Mrs Harris – she found her at eleven and ran like hell for another whisky before she could babble out what she found. Been treated ever since, she has, to embellish the whole story. Anyway, girl died about ten to ten-fifteen, as far as we can make out from the body reading and so on.'

'I wasn't far out in my preliminary calculation, then,' Tal said, with no feeling of satisfaction.

'No, not much. Nor with your suggestion about the cause of death. Strangulation, all right. Fierce grip, too – hell of a lot of bruising, and fracture of the carotid … but we're keeping the head, see, because of the wound at the back of the skull.' He pointed to the picture again. 'Just there. Nasty. Fracture, there. She got quite a thump and the police have brought in a brick which we've matched with the wound.'

'You mean she was struck down from behind with the brick?' Tal asked.

'Didn't say that,' Adams replied. 'Brick fragments and dust in the wound so she got clobbered with it all right, but it's not clear whether she was actually hit with the brick, or she *hit* the brick. You know, falling, like. Shoulders could have hit the ground, head jerking back, contact with the brick on the ground. Possible. If a lawyer asked me in court I'd have to express doubt.'

He screwed up his little eyes and stared thoughtfully at the photograph. 'Not the least of my doubts, though.'

'How do you mean?'

'Oh, plenty of circumstantial evidence, so that I could argue till the cows come home about lots of matters. But there's some funny things I can't prove, even though I got an experienced feelin' about them, if you know what I mean.'

'Such as?'

Adams pursed his lips, considering. 'Well, let's take the straightforward stuff first. We did a check, of course, on every inch of her body, every fibre of her clothing. So what did we get? First, we know she struggled with her assailant. She had a go at him; he thumped her in the face maybe before, maybe after she raked him with her nails. We got some flakes of skin from under three fingernails of her right hand.'

'Useful for identification,' Tal murmured.

'That's right. Okay, next thing is we got another pinpoint for the man who attacked her – he left a spot of blood on her shoulder, not much, very little really, but enough for us to go on. But then, the funny thing. No blood on her body. In fact, nothing *significant*. To start with, no evidence of semen.'

'So maybe he didn't get as far as raping her.'

'That's right. But let's look at facts. She's assaulted. Thumped. But no semen on her body, no blood other than her own, and no degree of bruising, on her thighs or on the vaginal wall.'

'But, surely–'

'Now, wait a minute, let me finish. Just get the picture. Bruised face, scratched heels, evidence of flailing arms, flakes of skin under the nails, spot of blood on the clothes, right? Then, underclothes ripped and torn away, blood on her thighs, a tear in the vaginal wall–'

'But you said–'

'Let me finish, damn it!' Adams glared indignantly at Tal. 'A tear, yes, blood, yes, but none of the bruising that would have occurred if she had been assaulted while she was still struggling and fighting a man off!'

'I'm not sure I understand what you're getting at,' Tal said slowly.

'I think you are. Wasn't a nice attack this, if any attack is nice. I wouldn't be able to prove this in court, other than in a negative way, Tal, but what it boils down to is this. The girl was clobbered. She was unconscious. She died. She was assaulted. She was strangled. We can prove all that. But I wouldn't like to have to prove the *sequence*.'

'You're suggesting–'

'I'm suggesting maybe this character strangled her first, and assaulted her afterwards. And though he did it violently, with his hands, it doesn't look as though she struggled much. Because she was dead.'

'In other words, maybe our friend is a necrophiliac,' the voice said from the doorway, and Tal turned to see Inspector Jack Arthur come forward. He wore a scowl on his face and his eyes glinted belligerently.

'Hello, Inspector,' Tal said.

'Here on business, then?'

'Partly social, partly professional, partly curiosity.'

'Aye.' Jack Arthur sniffed, and perched his broad bottom on the edge of Joe Adams' desk. 'Anything new?'

'Nothing except what was in the report to you.'

Arthur eyed Tal Rees truculently; he was in an evil humour. 'You got any new theories, Dr Rees?'

'No. Have you?'

'We're still looking for her lover.'

'And you still believe he's a married man?' Tal asked. Perhaps some of the tension in his voice was communicated to Arthur, who hesitated, watching him carefully. Then the policeman shook his head.

'We're keeping an open mind, like. I still think it's a lead we have to follow, but there's a few things...' He paused, as though considering whether he should divulge details of what had been found, but obviously assuming much of it would be common gossip shortly in any case, the valley being what it was, he went on. 'To start with, everything doesn't really fit in with that theory. The sexual assault, of course – why would her lover want to do that *after* she was unconscious, or even dead? And again, why would he tear open her handbag, take money – we think – from her purse, and throw both away? And if it was her lover, would he have had to battle with her the way he did?'

'She certainly put her nails on the man,' Joe Adams said.

'Aye... Anyway, we got things moving. We've started a door-to-door questioning, and now we're tracing all the people in the local pubs that night who might have walked past, or through, the Patch. Once we've got all the statements in we can do the necessary sifting. We'll pull in all the doubtful ones, and then we've got the prints from the handbag and the blood-stain to run tests against – but it all might not even be necessary, provided we can find the man before those scratches heal.'

'What about this blow on the head?' Tal asked.

'Not sure. Maybe he clobbered her with the brick, maybe she fell and struck her head. Not much difference, really. I mean, felony of violence, murder resulting ... it's all the same thing.'

He turned to Joe Adams with a sigh. 'Anyway, you got any coffee going?'

Adams nodded, reached under his desk, pulled out a percolator and plugged it into a socket in the wall. 'Can't stand that canteen stuff, even though this is against fire regulations. Cup for you, Tal?'

Tal shook his head. 'No, I'd better be on my way. We have another meeting of the Hospital Action Committee tonight, and I've got some rounds to do first.'

'Oh, aye,' Jack Arthur sneered. 'Still do-gooding, is it? Trouble is, from what I hear, there's a bit of do-badding in it as well these days.'

'What do you mean by that?' Tal asked.

Jack Arthur shrugged. 'I'm only going by what I hear. And read. The *Leader* wasn't very explicit yesterday, but there was a few hints. And the gossip in the valley is naming names. Like Maldwyn Powers.'

'Just what is the gossip saying?'

'Not very precise. The women on the corners just suggest that there's something funny been going on in the council. Oh, I know that's always the tale; occupational hazard it is, for a councillor. But this is a bit different in that they're talking about one councillor. Mal Powers. And he don't like it.'

'Has he taken it up with the police?'

'Nothing to take up, is there? I mean, gossip is gossip. We can't do a thing about it. But let's be clear where it started, Dr Rees.

With your partner, Evan Ritchie. I just hope he's got something to substantiate what he's saying.'

'I was there at the meeting,' Tal said carefully. 'I know what he said – and what he didn't. He certainly named no names.'

'But if the cap fits, is that it?' Jack Arthur said cheerfully. 'Still, I suppose that's how all you pressure-group characters work. Put a gentle boot in till the other chap begins to whimper, and then pretty soon you get your way. If the *police* adopt these tactics they get called thugs; but if the *cracach* do it, it's all right, isn't it? Funny world, you know; different standards for different people. And us coppers are bottom of the heap, believe me.'

Tal frowned. 'I think you're over-reacting to what Dr Ritchie said the other night. And as far as the rest of the committee is concerned, we had no idea what he was driving at – we weren't consulted previous to his speech.'

'Maybe. But no doubt the campaign will be successful – I mean, mud-slinging always helps because some of it is bound to stick. Maybe that's why Tommy Elias is changing his mind over the Cwmdare slag tip.'

'Is he?'

'So they say.'

'Who says?'

Jack Arthur grinned. 'The *valley* says. Damn, Dr Rees, you know that what the valley says today, *happens* tomorrow. Even if it wouldn't have happened if the valley hadn't said it. Events around here have a habit of following rumour – it's almost as though rumour makes the event. But do I have to tell you that?'

2

He had tramped these streets a thousand times. Long terraces whose backs faced the rising mountain, whose gutters were swept clean in the mid-morning by house-proud women, whose doorways displayed bright colours to contrast with the grey hewn stone of their walls. Tal had seen them in the early morning when the sheep came down to forage in the dustbins and late at night when young girls whispered goodnights to their sweethearts at darkened street corners. He had seen slates whirling from their roofs under violent winter winds and paper aircraft sailing among the chimneys on a light summer breeze. The revelry of a wake, the subdued excitement of a wedding, clarion calls from Methodist preachers and the red eyes of a pit widow in mourning, they were all part of the life he knew and existed within. Yet somehow he felt that he was drifting away from it, losing touch with the reality of it all. He went to see Lylie Jarman and she sat there in the deep armchair, crippled, with her arthritic fingers clasped around his and tears in her rheumy eyes. Her life had centred around her Da and when he died after thirty years of confinement to a wheelchair her own infirmities came to the surface, and she accepted her own pains. She clutched at Tal's hands as though her life lay in them and the image of God in Tal's eyes, but for Tal it didn't seem the same. He still felt the sadness and the sympathy; he still commiserated with her unmarried daughter who told him Lylie was still mourning after Da, but there was something missing inside him.

At Mrs Keegan's he delivered her third child. He listened to its cry and the thought came to him again – give it three hundred days of life and it would already have learned how to manipulate two adults with its wailing. He could look at the child and think again that there lay the potential of genius conceived in the darkness of blind desire, but somehow his thoughts were superficial, a repetition of long-spoken words, recreation of faded images.

For Tal, something was wrong with the valley.

But as he walked back to the surgery that evening and let himself into the lonely house he knew full well what lay at the root of his melancholy. Irresolution. He was cursed with an inability to reach the decision he knew, in his heart, was right for him. When he had buried himself in the valley, years ago, it had been to receive the comfort of a close, ordered existence in a world that had suddenly collapsed about him. And years later he had slowly come to realize that the valley had healed him and given him the capacity to love again. But he feared it, as he had feared the world outside the valley. And now he still feared it, and the strength of his own emotions.

It was all so simple really. Lyn would be leaving the practice in a matter of weeks. He could stop her – just by saying the right words. And she wanted him to say those words. But he could not – even though he saw the light in the valley fading, and the gathering hills grow dark about him.

Soon all that would be left for him was what Jack Arthur called 'do-gooding'.

He sat in the committee room of the Workmen's Institute and waited for the other members to come for the meeting of the Hospital Action Committee. He felt tired, and yet he should not have. He hadn't finished his round, had deliberately avoided going to the O'Haras', and Gwyneth Watkins, and the overman's widow, because he had felt he could face no more misery in the state of deep depression in which he found himself. But the lassitude that affected him seemed to have its effect upon his thinking too – he suddenly considered that the committee's work was so irrelevant, so unnecessary, so much shouting into a paper bag that he wanted to rise, leave, return home. He almost began to rise when the door opened, and the first of the committee arrived. Tal nodded as she wished him good evening and then the others trickled in.

When Lyn came in, there was only Evan Ritchie to come.

She seemed to stare very hard at Tal and her eyes glittered with a harsh, probing light, as though she were trying to look deep into his mind, strip away the defences that he had erected over the years. But this was mere fanciful imagining, for when she sat opposite him at the table there was a distant quality about her smile. He hadn't seen her since the night he had hurried from her home to examine the lifeless body of Barbara Porelli.

The chairman called the meeting to order and discussion began. Tal barely listened, though he tried to concentrate when he twice caught Lyn gazing at him with a tiny frown and professionally pursed lips – it was her diagnostic look and he had no desire to submit to diagnosis. She might find out things he did not want her to know.

He managed, vaguely, to keep up with the drift of the conversation. He got the impression they were playing for time, talking to little purpose, waiting for something to happen. They were going over old ground, reviewing the arguments that had come before the committee time and time again – the procedure for listed building consents, the application of the Town and Country Planning Acts and the new Control of Pollution Act to the proposals for the road through the valley, the need to plan their campaign to ensure maximum impact during the summer months so that the next meeting of council and planning committees should be placed under considerable public pressure. But it was not until the door opened, and Evan Ritchie walked into the room, that Tal realized just how much they had all been playing for time. It was Ritchie they wanted to hear, and the air of expectation lightened the atmosphere tangibly, there was a stir among the papers on the table, and even Tal felt a quickening of the pulse.

'My apologies, Mr Chairman,' Ritchie said brusquely. 'I've been down to Cardiff to see Ieuan James, and as a result I was rather late getting back home. I trust my absence had not incommoded you to any degree.'

My God, Tal thought, he's elevating his language in keeping with his sense of importance. But no one else seemed to notice. The chairman was gazing at Evan with ill-concealed interest.

'I think we'd all be interested to hear whether you were able to get any further information from Mr James,' he said portentously. Tal stared at Evan Ritchie with the others.

Ritchie was wearing a dark grey, carefully cut suit, pale yellow shirt and immaculately matched tie. His handsome features were composed, yet oddly excited, as though ripples of urgency ran under his skin like a fish slipping below the surface of a quiet river. His eyes were sharp, his hands controlled, but they had perhaps already betrayed a certain excitement in that he appeared to have cut himself while shaving, for a piece of flesh-coloured sticking plaster was placed along the line of his jaw.

'It was ... a useful meeting, Mr Chairman,' Evan Ritchie said.

The room waited expectantly as he paused, then raised the volume control so that his voice took on a sharp, almost stridently confident tone.

'You'll appreciate, Mr Chairman, that I'm in a position of some delicacy. Since I hinted at the public meeting that there might be ... ah ... submerged interests operating against us, I have been under some pressure from interested persons to speak more plainly. This, the law of defamation prevented me from doing, and it still prevents me from doing so.'

But everyone knows that you're talking about Mal Powers, Tal thought darkly.

'I have no compunction about stating that it is due to the advice and assistance of Ieuan James that I have managed to obtain the information I have,' Ritchie continued. He paused again, giving the committee time to appreciate that on their behalf he had been dealing with important people. 'As a result of conversations I have had with Mr James I was able to get in touch with the head of a building firm, and with a journalist working for a national daily. Both men were able to give me further information which, while not conclusive, yet reinforces my belief that this committee is facing not only sincerely held beliefs among our opponents, but also a certain amount of undeclared interest with a small group who hold positions of some influence.'

Tal looked at Lyn; the frown was still there, scarring her brow, but now it was directed not to him but to Evan Ritchie. She felt the way Tal did; Ritchie was saying nothing new so far, but merely reiterating veiled hints that were already causing damage to their opponents. It was not the sort of way she would have liked a campaign to be waged.

'Mr Chairman,' Lyn said suddenly, 'I for one would appreciate somewhat more explicit remarks from Mr Ritchie.'

The chairman glanced towards Evan, who contemplated his fingers, spread wide on the table in front of him. He seemed to give the impression that all the answers lay in those stubby, powerful fingers, but he was reluctantly compelled to retain that wisdom for the time being. He closed his fingers into fists.

'I've already stated that I'm in no position to name names, or even to define courses of action that have been taken. All I can do is raise questions, and ask that the proper bodies investigate the position. I touched upon these questions at the public meeting. With the information I now have at my disposal I'm prepared to make the challenges I then made more strident.'

He looked triumphantly around the expectant committee, but his eyes slipped past both Tal and Lyn, for he expected hostility in their eyes.

'The questions to be asked are these,' he said. 'Who on the Area Health Authority is outspoken against the project for the Llandarog Hospital? Second, what interests do the Road Project Committee have in building firms in Clwyd? Third–'

'Now wait a minute,' Tal interrupted. 'The fact that some members of the Area Health Committee are against our arguments is no–'

'Order,' snapped the chairman, 'order, please … Mr Ritchie?'

'The third question concerns the local planning committee,' Evan said smoothly, refusing to meet Tal's angry glance. 'We all know the membership of that committee. What we do not know is how voting has gone in that committee over the last eighteen months–'

'I'm sorry, Mr Chairman,' Tal interrupted

again, 'but that is a matter of public record, and Mr Ritchie should say what he means. Has *he* looked up the voting record? If so, any conclusions he draws should be stated here. For God's sake, all we're getting is innuendo, and I don't like it. Our function–'

'I'm quite aware of our function and our beliefs,' Ritchie said sharply, colour staining his face and making the sticking plaster on his jaw stand out by contrast. 'As for the voting being a matter of public record, that's so – and it has been checked.'

'By you?'

'It has been checked. I want it checked by the proper authorities. Now, may I go on? Llandarog House is a listed building. The planning committee has to go through an authorized procedure before any demolition or construction or alteration can go on in relation to that building. Moreover, we must also point to the structure plan for the area. It has not yet been published in its entirety. It is true that local councillors are expressly advised not to deal officially with decision-taking over structure plans until the public has been allowed to participate in the planning, through the medium of community forums or public meetings and representations and so on, but what I want to ask is whether the chairman of the local planning committee–'

'Mal Powers,' Tal interrupted. 'Let's name names.'

Evan Ritchie's eyes glittered. 'Whether the chairman of the local planning committee has scrupulously followed the principles laid down as far as procedures are concerned. And whether he has declared all interests he has which might affect the result of decisions taken in committee.'

He waited, as though expecting another interruption from Tal Rees. When it did not come, he added shortly and distinctly, 'And finally, I would like to know what influenced certain members to change sides in the arguments during committee meetings.'

'The power of the other side's arguments, perhaps,' Tal sneered. 'But you want us to consider the question whether they'd been bought off, I suppose?'

'I don't know what's getting into you, Tal,' Ritchie said, ignoring the chairman.

'I don't like smear campaigns. If you've got evidence of corruption bring it out, but don't talk vaguely about it.'

'There is evidence.'

'But you've not got it!'

'Dr Rees, whose side are you on?' the chairman asked acidly.

'I'm not on the side of a group of individuals who seem to be using McCarthyite
tactics to smear a man who has been of long
service to this community but who happens
to be opposed to the principles in which we
believe over the matter of Llandarog Hospital,' Tal said, scraped his chair back, and
walked out of the room. He was cold, but the
room was colder.

The river was different now.

There was a time when its shallow waters
had been black with coal-dust, and the fish
had fled, their gills choked with the black
death. When Tal was young little boys had
been able to see tiddlers only in the tiny
tributary streams that trickled down the
mountainside, and though trout still throve
in the feeder dams constructed above the pits
for cooling purposes, and in the banked
pools under the trestle timber weirs that led
down towards the pitheads, even they had
gone eventually, as the pits closed, feeders
were dynamited, and banks became silted up.

But now the river was clean again. Some
people swore they had seen salmon up at
Treharne, and trout had certainly returned
in small numbers under the banks. The
pebbles were discernible again, as they had

been only on Bank Holidays at one time, but they were clean pebbles now, not the oily kind the old valley had held. But even those old pebbles had gleamed under the moon, as the white ones did now.

The wire suspension of the bridge trembled and sang softly as a light step came to the planking. Tal still leaned on the rail and stared down at the gleaming water slipping away, chuckling, to the sea, as the footsteps came nearer and the bridge began to dance gently, swinging in a long lifting movement, in time with the walker on its timbers. The footsteps drew near and stopped; the bridge sighed, slowed its shivering dance, and was quiet. The river gurgled away and under the far bank a water rat splashed.

'I thought I might find you here,' Lyn said softly.

'Peaceful.'

'Like always...' Tal knew what she meant. He had been coming here for thirty years, after all, and when he was disturbed, this long way around home, crossing the river once by the iron bridge and a second time by this suspension bridge, gave him time to stop and think and come to terms with himself again.

'What is the matter, Tal?'

He shook his head. It was so many things. 'I don't know. Menopausal man, perhaps. Life just seems to have … changed. Maybe it's the fact you've decided to leave the practice and you know I hate things changing like that. Maybe it's Barbara Porelli's death. Maybe it's Evan and his ambitions, or the dirty campaign he and Ieuan James seem to be starting, or maybe it's the thought of Cwmdare or perhaps it's just that I'm getting old. I really don't *know*, Lyn. I feel, somehow, that I ought to be taking decisions, but I don't know what they are or what they should be.'

'You need worry no longer about whether you should get involved in Cwmdare, anyway,' Lyn said quietly. 'It's been settled.'

Tal raised his head and looked at her. She was standing perhaps six feet away from him, leaning against the rail, and her face was pale in the moonlight, her hair jet black and smooth.

'I'd heard something about it,' he said.

'It seems as though Tommy Elias costed it all up, weighed the price he might have to pay for a protracted battle with the Trust, and finally instructed his solicitors to pay a sum by way of compensation to the Trust for the loss of the cottages. I gather there will now be a motion before the council at the next meeting to clear a site further up the cwm so that some purpose-built cottages and play areas can be constructed for the Trust – using the money furnished by Elias. The Trust's campaign at least seems to have paid off.'

'I'm still surprised,' Tal said. 'I would never have thought Tommy Elias would have given in that way.'

'Money talks.'

'You're beginning to sound like Evan.' The moment he had said it, Tal regretted it, but after a short silence, when Lyn spoke she seemed to have taken no offence.

'What do you think about this Mal Powers thing, Tal? After you walked out there was an embarrassed silence, and Evan made a short speech about people being out of touch with reality, unwilling to face facts, and the meeting folded a bit abruptly. I think a number of the committee are some-what uneasy the way things are going.'

'I'm more than just uneasy,' Tal said. 'I consider that Evan is going about this thing in entirely the wrong way. We have been arguing along environmental issues up till now – and we've had a strong case. It's difficult to be objective, I know, but I've felt all along that we could win through on these grounds. But now, suddenly, we're changing our tack – or Evan is changing it for us. The whole flavour of the campaign is different. Evan has started out on a witch hunt, and whether he's actually naming Mal Powers or not he is certainly raising clouds of dust which will bring trouble – and cause more than a few accidents.'

'How do you mean?'

'Dammit, Lyn, you know what I mean. You know how things are in the valley! A sniff of gossip and the odour will cling to you for the rest of your life. If a bit of scandal slaps a name on you, people will eventually forget what it was all about in the first place but the name will stick. And soon exaggerations arise, legends will grow up and in the end you hardly recognize the fact behind the rumour. If Evan goes on the way he is Mal Powers will go down as the most corrupt councillor the valley has ever seen.'

'But that's just nonsense. His record of service–'

'His record of service will matter not a damn. It won't even matter if he ever was corrupt, if the rumours take hold. And that's another thing I don't like about it. It's not only the fact that Evan is changing the nature of our campaign, it's the suspicion that we are talking about nothing. What have we got so far? Nothing concrete, for sure. Ieuan James is invited up here to lend his support to the hospital campaign. He casually mentions suggestions of corruption on the part of one of our sternest opponents. Now he may be right, he may be wrong. After all, James works in the building industry, and there's more than a few bribes flying around there. James himself, for instance, he's a big enough businessman to have paid out more than a few kick-backs himself. The cynical among us might even argue he couldn't win the contracts he had done without indulging in a fair amount of bribery and corruption himself. But it's Evan's reaction which upsets me. He seizes on James's words, expands on them, dashes off to Cardiff to interview James's sources, as far as I can gather. But what do we get as a result? Still nothing but innuendo. Damn, *bach,* it's not good enough. You can't go around the place spreading malicious hints about people without eventually coming up with facts to prove your allegations!'

'Evan insists he's making no allegations, as yet,' Lyn said doubtfully. 'At least, he argues that he's named no one, simply asked questions that deserve answers.'

'Oh, aye, he's asked questions, but the

important thing is what people think are the reasons behind the questions! All right, he's made no positive allegations. I grant him that. He can't be nailed for slander, for he has named no one publicly – it's only Ieuan James actually gave out Mal Powers's name. Where other people picked it up is a matter of doubt – unless James has leaked the name for reasons of his own. I can't see what they might be. No matter, the fact is that the name is being bandied about. And if Evan never takes it any further than that he'll be in no trouble. On the other hand, Mal Powers could be.'

Lyn shivered slightly. She moved closer to Tal, leaning on the rail, staring down into the shining water below them. There was a brief, phosphorescent gleam as something broke the surface near the bank, a splashing sound as an inhabitant of the river bank slipped into the water, and far upstream, under the curve of the hill, an owl hooted, melancholy and distant, its call drifting along the swing of the river, fading under the banks and the trees, dying against the backs of terraced houses.

'I don't understand,' Lyn said, shaking her head. 'If Evan doesn't take the matter any further, if he doesn't come up with any facts that will back up these allegations, these hints, call them what you will, what will be the point of the whole exercise?'

'Think of it this way, Lyn. There's Mal Powers, sitting on these committees, with the support of his fellow councillors, against us, but with a substantial minority against him and for us. Rumours start to go the rounds, the valley begins to whisper. You know as well as I do that a valley whisper is like a bugle on a clear day. Can't you see what'll happen? All those worthies from the chapel who'll say wisely that there's no smoke without a bonfire somewhere, and pretty soon a couple of those councillors who support Mal will be edging away from him in the chamber, or just not turning up to vote. It doesn't matter whether Mal Powers is guilty of corruption or not – every official in the valley is *assumed* to be corrupt, for why else does anyone go into local government? Once a whisper starts *particularizing, myna fyrny,* everyone knows the man in question must be guilty. And friends are suddenly not friends.'

'You think that's what is behind all this?'

Tal nodded. A note of disgust crept into his voice. 'I think Evan has no hard information about Maldwyn Powers. I think he's just using this as a means of getting the planning decision reversed in our favour.

157

Oh, maybe there is a little fire under the smoke – we all have some secrets to hide – but I'm convinced Evan is sacrificing Mal Powers deliberately.'

'And making his political name?' Lyn asked softly.

Tal hesitated. To agree would almost be to do what he was criticizing Evan for doing: muddying a man's name without proof. But Lyn had already said it once, and Tal was now inclined to agree with her assessment of their partner in the practice. 'Yes. Maybe there's a bit of politicking in it too.' Bitterly, he added, 'It seems to me that perhaps the wrong person is leaving the practice.'

Lyn was silent. They stood there for several minutes in the soft moonlight, and the hills crouched about them, round-shouldered, hunched, eavesdropping on their subdued conversation. At last, she said in a voice that was steeled with a defensiveness he had never noted before, 'That won't do, Tal. Even if you decided to break with Evan, it would make no difference as far as I was concerned. The decision has been taken by both of us. My staying in the practice would solve nothing. Not now.'

He knew what she meant. And he knew the words that could change things radically. But he could not say them. They trembled on his lips, but he could not bring them forth. Next moment the chance was gone. More briskly, Lyn said, 'However, it's not just this I wanted to see you about. I gather you haven't heard the news?'

His mind was in a turmoil, and he hardly heard what she said.

'No one seems to have seen him for days, and I only heard this evening, just before the meeting, that he'd been arrested. They took him down to Pontypridd for questioning, but the story is that he's already admitted the whole thing. I thought at first, in the meeting, when I saw you looking so down and depressed, that you'd heard; I realized then that if you had heard you'd probably not have stayed for the meeting. Then ... well, I've been reluctant to tell you in a way. I'm still ... shocked, disbelieving myself ... I just can't bring myself to accept that–'

'What are you talking about?' Tal asked, like a man coming out of a dream.

'Barbara Porelli,' Lyn said in an impatient tone. 'They've arrested him for her murder. But I just can't believe–'

'Colin Owen?'

Lyn stared at Tal open-mouthed.

'Who? What are you talking about?

Haven't you been *listening* to me, Tal? Jack Arthur has taken the line that he now has the man responsible for the murder of Barbara Porelli on the Patch. But not Colin Owen!'

'Then who, *bach*, who are you talking about?'

'Mr Jones,' she hissed at him impatiently. 'You know – *Willy Thatch!*'

3

It was two in the morning when Tal arrived at the police station in Pontypridd, to be told that Inspector Jack Arthur had left instructions that he was to be kept waiting until the inspector himself arrived. Since Tal had had considerable difficulty in obtaining permission from the Chief Constable even to visit the station, Arthur's embargo upon his seeing Willy Thatch until Arthur had arrived was frustrating but hardly surprising.

Nor was Jack Arthur's appearance surprising. He came into the room, where Tal had been left with a cool cup of tea, at almost three in the morning. His eyes were bloodshot and angry, his jowls shaded with a dark stubble, and he looked thoroughly bad-tempered. In a more reasonable frame of mind Tal might have felt sympathy with him, but right now Tal was so angry and incensed at the muddle-headedness of the police that he was in no state to feel anything other than fury at Jack Arthur and all his band.

'Now what the hell is this all about?' Arthur growled.

'You took the words right out of my mouth,' Tal retorted sharply, and was rewarded by daggers of hatred from Jack Arthur's eyes. For a moment he thought the inspector was about to strike him: with fists balled at his sides, Arthur gradually controlled himself. He took a deep breath.

'Now then, Dr Rees. I'll try to keep calm. I been workin' on this case for several days and me and my men are tired as hell. We been trampin' all over the valley, down on our hands and knees scrabblin' in dirt, fishin' in rivers, muckin' about in all the most horrible places you can imagine. We been asking questions; we been reading statements till our eyes have all but popped up; we been checking and cross-checking and cross-cross-checking over and bloody over again until the sun gets up, while all you kind of people are tucked up safe in bed wonderin' why the hell it takes the coppers so long to get the man who killed Barbara Porelli. And then, when we get him, and I try to get a couple of hours kip, the bloody Chief Constable phones me and tells me I'd better get down here because some bloody fool of a medic wants to get in to see Willy Thatch. What's the matter, you go to school with the Chief Constable or something?'

'That's about it. And I know Willy Thatch, too,' Tal snapped. 'And you're barking up the wrong tree entirely.'

'Now is that so?' Jack Arthur sneered. 'So what tree should we be barkin' up – and why haven't you been around to point it out before? Bloody *amateurs!*'

Tal almost knocked over his teacup as he rose abruptly to his feet. He pointed an accusatory finger at Jack Arthur. 'Amateur or not, I know it when you're making a fool of yourself. Moreover, I know why you've pulled in Willy Thatch. There are some people in the valley you can trample all over, and he's one of them. All right, he's no good, but he's weak and he'd fold up inside as soon as you put any pressure on him. This is nothing more than a political move, Inspector Arthur, and I'm fed up to the back teeth with politics!'

Arthur looked at him with real amazement in his eyes. 'What the hell you on about?'

'You're charging Willy Thatch because

you're panicked that you'll never get the real murderer! You've got a reputation to save, and this is your way of doing it! You grab the first helpless victim you can find, one who can't fight back, and you'll pin the whole thing on him to your satisfaction, irrespective of the fact that you've got an innocent man in that cell!'

Jack Arthur sat down suddenly and positively. He stared at Tal Rees and his own anger was dying. His eyes were careful, his gaze contemplative; he sat there staring at Tal, weighing up what was behind his outburst, attempting to calculate how far he should go in what he was about to say. If there were any violent words in his mind he quelled them, held them back; Taliesin Rees was well known in the community and well respected. It wasn't a good thing to get tough with a doctor who had lived high in people's regard for almost thirty years in the valley. With a face carved into impassivity Jack Arthur nodded.

'We'd better talk this out, Dr Rees. Calmly.'

Tal stood foolishly, his hand still extended, his finger pointed. What the hell was he playing at? He must be tired, overwrought. He reached for the chairback, sat down across the table from Jack Arthur. His hand was trembling.

'You all right, Doctor?' Arthur said coldly.

'I'm all right. It's Willy Thatch I'm concerned about.'

Jack Arthur's gaze became owlish. 'So what's your complaint?'

'You've got the wrong man – you *must* have!'

'Why do you say that?'

Tal took a deep breath. 'I know Willy Thatch; I've known him for years. He's a drunken ex-miner whose last job was as a storekeeper in Treforest, and he's not held down a regular job for years. He's bald and he's ugly and he's got a wife and eight kids and he scrounges off the State. I know all that. I know too that he spends almost all he gets on beer in the Alexandra Hotel, leaving Mrs Jones with a pittance to bring up those children. Willy Thatch is big, argumentative, self-indulgent, with a mind that blanks out in drink and becomes wheedling in sobriety. I know all that – as most people do. But I know more than that, as well.'

Jack Arthur fished in his pocket and drew out a battered packet of cigarettes. He took out one cigarette, inspected its filter, glanced at Tal and then replaced the cigarette with an unhappy frown.

'If you know more, you'd better tell me about it.'

'Rightly or wrongly, Willy Thatch genuinely feels himself to be one of the valley's unfortunates. He's got a good wife but he sees her as the reason for his misfortunes over the years. If she hadn't been so fertile–'

'It was *he* saddled her with the kids!'

'I know that, but I'm simply explaining how he rationalizes his own weaknesses. He blames her for his inability to make a career for himself – though God knows what he could ever have done by way of a *career*. But because of what he sees as an unfortunately early marriage and a fruitful wife with whom he has been burdened, he seeks strength and solace and the regard of his companions in drink. It's true he then finds more problems than he's leaving behind, but the fact is he's a moral and social coward; he lacks touch with reality; when he's sober he's open to suggestion; but he's no more capable of murdering a young woman like Barbara Porelli than I am.'

Jack Arthur inspected his fingernails. 'I think you have something to add to all that – about us, for instance?'

Tal hesitated. 'Maybe I was a bit ... impulsive in my earlier remarks. But I insist that you've got the wrong man. Willy Thatch isn't capable of killing the way that girl was killed.'

'When I came in you suggested we were fixing Willy Thatch because he could *be* fixed. You imputed motives to me and my men that are, to say the least, dishonest and criminal. What about your motives, Dr Rees? Why are you so strong, rushing in here?'

'I don't want to see an innocent man accused of a crime.'

'But how do you *know* he's innocent? What *really* brought you here?'

Tal felt his stomach surge. It was a question he had not yet faced up to: was he here because of a sense of guilt, or because of Colin Owen ... or for a whole range and mixture of confused and confusing reasons? He saw Jack Arthur raise a dismissive hand, wave the question away with a three o'clock-in-the-morning weariness.

'No matter. I'm too bloody tired to argue about it, anyway. I want to get home to bed. But before I do, the Chief Constable tells me I have to satisfy you that everything's as it should be. Apparently your work as a pressure group specialist and a respected medic in the community hold water with him if not with me. So you can see your beloved drunk. But before you do, there's a few things I have to say.' He hunched himself forward, placing his elbows on the table and glaring at Tal. There was a real malice in his voice and in his eyes. 'I saw you down at the forensic laboratories and you got the background picture. You might as well have it all now. To begin with, we didn't pull Willy Thatch in at random because he's weak and a drunk. It was all part of an organized procedure. We were doing a house-to-house; checking and cross-checking, like I said before. And one of the things we checked on was people who would have been walking the street about the time that girl died.'

'There would have been a hundred people–'

'We checked them all, all we could find. But in our questioning of people in the pubs we worked on a pattern. You know it was Mrs Harris who found the corpse. She came out of the Duke of Monmouth, you remember? We talked to everyone who was in there that night. And we did the same with the clientele of the White Hart, and that left just one more pub in the near vicinity.'

'The Alexandra Hotel.'

'That's right. The Alex. Now when we talked to the regulars there, funny thing. We heard that Willy Thatch had been in most of the evening, but spent himself out, tried to cadge a few bob, got stroppy so they threw him out. At quarter to ten. Next thing was, no one had seen him since.'

'His wife–'

'His wife is in hospital, and he's not been near her. We checked. So, okay, we eventually get around to calling on Willy. He didn't want to see us. When we insisted, and all but forced our way in, we found out the reason for his reluctance. He hadn't shaved for a couple of days.'

'I don't see–'

'He hadn't shaved,' Arthur said heavily, 'because he wanted to grow a beard. It would help cover the scratches on his face.'

The words died away and Tal stared foolishly at Inspector Jack Arthur. The pathologist had said there were flakes of skin under Barbara's nails. She had torn at her attacker's face. Scratches... People often got scratched ... a piece of sticking plaster along a jawline...

'It was just a start, of course,' Arthur said. 'And like you said, Willy Thatch is weak, open to suggestion. But we didn't *suggest* anything to him, just asked him a few questions about his face and his wanderings that night, pointed out that his route home ran straight past the Patch and said that he might have seen the girl – and then it all came out.'

'What do you mean?'

'Confession!'

'He confessed? I don't believe it.'

'You'd better believe it,' Arthur said curtly. 'We got it all down on paper and signed, no pressure.'

Tal shook his head. 'I can't–'

'Now wait a minute, Doctor.' Jack Arthur's eyes were shimmering with suppressed anger suddenly. 'It's time you got a few things straight. We got one hell of a case against Willy Thatch – I'm not stupid enough to risk my career by hauling in someone I'm not *sure* killed Barbara Porelli. But for your benefit, so you don't make a fool of yourself squealing up and down the valley about injustice, I'll put you in the picture. We got it down in writing. Willy Thatch came out of that pub at quarter to ten. He staggered on his way home. He saw Barbara Porelli near the Patch and he followed her. He tussled with her on the waste ground and tried to interfere with her, as the Sundays say. She put up a struggle and so he brained her with a brick. She went down, he tore some of her clothing away, and tried to have it off with her. He was unsuccessful; he pulled at her with his hands, but when he tried to go further he was so

169

shaken and excited he'd finished before he'd even started, and all he did was stain some of her clothing. It was then that she started to come around, and when she opened her mouth to yell for help he grabbed her by the throat. He strangled her. Then he got up, picked up her purse, stole what little money she had, threw away her purse and handbag, shambled off home. He was still capable enough to realize that with scratches on his face he couldn't go into a pub, so he bought a bottle in an off-licence in Thomas Street, keeping his face averted, went home, got soused on her money, and then decided he'd better stay home until his face fungus grew. But he was shaking scared, man, I'll tell you that!'

'He said all this?' Tal asked incredulously.

'Most of it. Some we had to piece together. But don't get uppity with me, Dr Rees; even the bits we have to piece together won't be the roughest parts. The main stuff we got from him. And there'll be corroborative evidence. I'm confident that when forensic check the scratches they'll come up with evidence to prove the skin under the girl's nails was Willy Thatch's. And it's my guess a blood check will produce a similar result.'

'But I can't believe that Willy Thatch

would have the necessary ... *drive* to behave in this way,' Tal said helplessly.

'He was shoved along by two of the oldest drives in the world,' Arthur replied. 'You got to remember, Dr Rees, he'd just got thrown out of a pub. He had no money; and money is the route to popularity for men like Willy Thatch. No one would *give* it to him, so he had to take it. Who easier to take it from than a girl walking by herself? And the other drive was just as important – maybe even more important. You know as well as I do that Willy Thatch has never been a man to deny himself the physical pleasures of life. But he's *been* denied for weeks. And with his wife in hospital, there was no prospect of relief. Until he saw Barbara Porelli walking down towards the Patch. I don't know; it's not clear even to him whether he went after her for sexual relief or money, in the first instance. All we do know is that he tried to obtain both. And Barbara Porelli died. So you still want to tell me I've pulled in the wrong man?'

Tal was silent for a moment. He sat staring at his hands, trying to envisage Willy Thatch attacking Barbara Porelli, and somehow it was impossible to grasp as a mental image.

'I'd like to see him.'

'To make sure we haven't brutalized him?'

Arthur mocked. 'To make sure we haven't knocked him around, kicked his teeth down his throat, forced him to write a confession? Damn, we didn't need to, man; he was a lamb, a weeping lamb full of the joys of remorse! But you can see him all right; far be it from me to prevent you chatting with your poor, poor Willy Thatch!'

Arthur picked up the phone, rang through to the duty desk, told the constable there to arrange for Willy Thatch to be brought out of the cells for Dr Rees's inspection. He replaced the phone, smiled a twisted smile at Tal and settled back in his chair.

'I suppose you'll say I'm cruel dragging him out of his kip now – but you dragged me out of mine, didn't you? Ah … you're all the same, you bloody do-gooders. Squeal like hell over the worthless ones like Willy Thatch, the mindless, brutal scroungers who plunge away self-indulgently and then cry when the consequences leap in their faces. All the same, you are. What you ought to be asking is about the others. The ones who die. That girl, she was one of your patients, wasn't she? Been to see you, hadn't she? Why don't you ask yourself now what you could have done for *her*?'

Tal's face was stiff, his mouth set in a thin

line. He tried to wash his mind clean but Arthur's words remained in his consciousness, part of a tangled jungle of incomprehension, thickets of doubt, confusions of motivations and actions. He came to with a start when the door opened suddenly.

Jack Arthur was equally surprised – and angry. He opened his mouth to swear at the young constable who had entered so abruptly, but the words died on his lips as he saw the man's white face.

'Inspector...'

There was a pause. Arthur stood up. 'What's the matter?'

'You'd better come–'

Arthur strode from the room, and was half way down the corridor before he suddenly turned, after a brief consultation with the constable, and yelled back to Tal.

'Dr Rees! You'd better come with us.'

Arthur was running when Tal came out of the doorway.

They had cut him down before Tal arrived. The old leather belt displayed a clean edge where the knife had shorn through it, in marked contrast to the worn, stained surface of the leather. The buckle was tight drawn against the throat and had cut deeply into the flesh. Bulging eyes, a tongue forced between clenched teeth, a trickle of blood from the corner of the mouth. Tal knelt over the body to make a quick examination. There was no flutter of a pulse, no sign of life.

'Ambulance?'

'Sent for.'

Tal rocked back on his heels. It was all pointless. An hour, two hours ago...

Willy Thatch looked immense in his striped pyjamas – bigger than he had seemed in life. Tal could not help thinking of the man as he had been, and Barbara Porelli.

'Well, at least we got a bit more evidence to check with,' Jack Arthur said hoarsely. When Tal looked up, surprised, Arthur pointed to the stain on the front of the dead man's trousers. 'The last one he wouldn't have wanted, or expected...'

The disgust must have shown in Tal's eyes, because Jack Arthur's eyes snapped away and a little colour returned to his face. He bit his lip.

'He's dead, I suppose?'

'Yes.'

Jack Arthur took a deep breath and swore, a string of involved, juvenile oaths. Tal stood impassively, listening but not hearing. An hour or two, and this might not have happened. Mrs Jones, in Church Village...

'God, what a mess,' Jack Arthur said. 'Well, now we're for it, lads. Get rid of one problem, and then we got one a bloody sight bigger!'

CHAPTER IV

For the next few days life was a mechanical exercise for Taliesin Rees. He ate, he worked, he slept badly; he went on his rounds, tended to his patients, doled out prescriptions and made noises that sounded like sympathy, but inside him there was an emptiness he had experienced only once before, years ago. The valley had given him his life then, but he knew it could not do it twice. He tried to fight against it in the desperate lonely darkness hours but it settled upon him like a vast black crow – the conviction that he had failed as a doctor and as a human being.

He tried to explain it to Lyn.

'Can't you understand? I can be a success here in this valley if I *feel*, if my commitment is an emotional, sensitive understanding one. I told you this years ago when you decided to work in the valley – it isn't enough merely to practise medicine and dispense drugs; you must be *part* of the people here. And that means you must know them, and live a part of their lives for them and with them.'

'And you've done that, Tal!' she had interrupted fiercely.

'I *thought* I had done it! But I thought I knew Willy Thatch! And I thought I had sympathy for his wife, down there in Church Village. But how can I face her now, when her eyes will ask me why I never went near Willy at the house while she was in hospital? Can I say I was too busy, when he was there, cowering in the back room, desperately trying to grow a beard to hide scratch marks on his face? How can I answer her when her eyes tell me that if I *had* gone to see him he could have explained to me, not to the police, and maybe it would all have been cleared up. Maybe Willy would never have been arrested. Maybe, then, he would never have found himself in a lonely terrifying cell, with a guilt hanging over him that drove him to kill himself!'

'If he killed Barbara Porelli–'

'I can't believe he did! Lyn, it sounds so plausible, and seems to fit the facts Jack Arthur puts forward, but I knew him! Stupid, even belligerent, but he wouldn't have killed her deliberately! He might have tried to assault her – all right, but she could have fallen, struck the back of her head – I can't then believe he would have *strangled* her.'

'The police are taking inquiries no further, Tal.'

'And I know why! It's all so neat for them – and Jack Arthur's got a bigger worry on his head. He and the rest of them, they've got all their work cut out to try to explain how it was a man hanged himself in their cells. They've got an official inquiry to face and they're scared to death. They'll come out of it with a finding of negligence, no doubt – the last thing they want now is something to show that the man who killed himself in that cell wasn't even guilty of the crime with which he was charged.'

'The confession–'

'Willy Thatch was a weak man, a coward both morally and socially. He was scared, with hazy memories of what happened, and wide open to suggestion! If only I had gone to see him, kept my promise to his wife, if I had been first to talk to him, rather than Jack Arthur! Can't you see it, Lyn? Can't you see how I've failed?'

She refused to see it. She saw only an over-reaction on his part, a self-indulgence, even.

He had been under too much strain, she said. When did he last take a holiday? Two years ago, as far as she could remember.

To hell with holidays. Tal had his guilts, and maybe they were rooted in a darkened past that was chapel-ridden, and suffocating, and held memories of his father's leather belt, the dark serge of his father's knee pressed hard against his face, but Freudian nonsense of that kind could not serve now to release him from his numb sense of failure.

There was only his work, but that was done mechanically and without heart. And if that was the way of it, there was nothing left.

On the mountain, the sheep sometimes raised a harsh racking sound that seemed to tear the heart from them, rip away the linings of their throat, slash open their lungs. That coughing sound was well known to Tal, but he heard it now in the chest of Dai Ponies. As he wrote out a prescription, Tal glanced up at the old man, buttoning the flimsy shirt over his meagre chest.

'This prescription isn't the answer, Dai, only part of it.'

'Don't want to hear what you're goin' to say, Dr Rees,' Dai Ponies said with a wheeze in his chest.

'I'm going to say it, nevertheless. When was it you came down to see me last, Dai?'

The wrinkled face screwed up in concentration. 'Seven years, I suppose it was. Time I broke my ankle, I think.'

'And you set that damned thing yourself, or tried to. It's no good, Dai, you'll have to come down from that mountain.'

'Can't do that, Dr Rees.'

'You won't last the winter out. Summer now, and you've got a hell of a chest.'

Dai Ponies chuckled. 'Maybe so, but better to die up there than be shoved in prison up at 'Ceiber. That's what it is, prison.'

'It's an Old People's Home,' Tal said calmly.

'Prison.'

'You'd keep alive there.'

'Livin' death,' Dai Ponies said wickedly, grinning at Tal. 'Can't make me go, you can't.'

'I wouldn't try. But you'll have to live in a drier place, Dai. You've got bronchitis, and you need to be warm and dry and well-fed. At Penceiber–'

'Bugger 'Ceiber. Don't need it. I'll outlive most of them; you too, Dr Rees. Outlived a good few already. Teddy Jenkins has gone now. Sam Williams Shop too. And then there's Willy Thatch. Outlived him, haven't

I? Soft bugger, he was, mind.'

Tal frowned. Dai Ponies was watching him with cunning old eyes, sharp with the wisdom of the hills.

'What do you mean by that, Dai?'

'Soft. Hangin' hisself. Soft, that was. Could talk him into anythin', you could. No doubt they did.'

'Do you know anything about that, Dai?'

'Me? No, only a bit of gossip, that's all. Always gossip on the mountains, you know; sort of comes whispering up from the back lanes and the gullies, see. Funny, it is. But if you listen hard enough, you hear it all, you do. About Willy Thatch, and the chemist down at Trefowydd, and Mal Powers–'

'You've heard gossip about Maldwyn Powers?' Tal asked.

Dai finished buttoning his shirt before he answered. He slipped his skinny arms into the decrepit jacket he had draped over the back of the chair while Tal had examined him, and he nodded, a curious nodding that seemed to begin at his waist so that his whole body moved stiffly in a ritual dance.

'Few words here, few words there, gossip here, chat there, eh, all these women on the street corners and men in the clubs they don't hear the half of it. Whispers come up the mountain all the time. Why, I remember twenty years ago...'

Tal had often wondered where the old man got his information, but wherever it came from it was always current gossip interspersed with ancient tales, a kind of moralizing by comparison, except that the old days always seemed to have been more exciting, more moral, more sinful, depending which particular piece of gossip Dai Ponies was retailing at the time.

'Mal Powers, you said.'

'Oh, aye...' Dai squinted wisely at Tal and cocked his head to one side. 'Not *valley* gossip, you know.'

'How do you mean?'

'Come from outside, this has.'

'How do you know that?'

'Different feel. I been listening on the mountain for thirty years, Dr Rees. Know the feel and taste of valley gossip. This is different. Malicious, like. Valley gossip, it's got malice, of course, but *family* malice. Not this talk. Different, it is.'

'In what way, exactly?'

'Got a purpose, it has. Most gossip is just gossip – Mrs Ardwyn doin' a bit of dirty on Father Kelly, that sort of thing – but this isn't really gossip at all, the Mal Powers talk. It's as though it's put about for a reason that's got nothing to do with the valley, really.'

Tal frowned. He turned away and began to wash his hands. He watched the old man in the mirror; Dai's eyes never left Tal's back.

'I don't understand what you mean.'

'Ah, well, there you are, Dr Rees. Perhaps I don't really understand it myself, you know. But it's about bribin', isn't it? Plenty of bribery in the valley, of course. Famous for it, it is. Old Mathias the Minister at Bethesda Chapel now, he was a great one for it – got a new chapel out of the coal-owners and 'Ceiber, he did, for agreeing to sell up a piece of land he held on the north side of the valley. Bribery, wasn't it? For the satisfaction of the Lord, he said, though he had a good price for his land as well, mind. And there was old Rest-Day Elias, now, he did more than his fair share of linin' pockets to get his own way. Tale is, his son isn't any better. But Mal Powers, now, there's such a thing…'

'What credence should we put on such stories, Dai?' Tal asked, with a tiny voice inside him crying disgust that he should encourage Dai Ponies to retail slanderous stories in his presence. Perhaps the old man heard the echo of that voice, because some of the glitter went from his eyes.

'Credence? I don't know. Mathias story is true. Elias story can be vouched for. But Mal Powers, I told you, it isn't valley gossip, and so I can't feel it, and can't tell you whether it's true or not. Most times, smoke and fire, but I wouldn't trust this story. Truth is always a bit difficult to come by, isn't it, and though I think people will say Mal Powers might have got his fingers sticky once or twice, so what about it? Chairman of the Co-op Committee, wasn't he? Damn, that's what a man takes that job for. Help the people, and help himself.'

'This talk is a bit more serious than a bag of sugar and a slice of cheese, Dai.'

'Aye. But talk's cheap. I mean, even Willy Thatch talked cheap, didn't he? Stupid bugger. Now that girl, she'd never have been Willy's cup of tea, would she, not really? And she wasn't a Patch kind of girl either. I mean, in the old days she was up the mountains like all the rest of the young 'uns, but from what they say she lived it up a bit in Cardiff, none of this standin' up in a dark corner of the Patch, is it?'

Tal stared at the old man for a long moment, and Dai Ponies met his glance un-winkingly. Tal frowned. 'I don't quite understand what you mean, Dai,' he said.

'Mean? Don't mean nothin', I don't. Just a fact, isn't it? That girl was past the stage when she'd have dropped her knickers down on waste ground like the Patch. If she ever went through that stage. Mountain now, under a hot sun, different that is, catches them all, that does, and I seen her as bad as others in the old days, but the Patch, no, she didn't go down there for that, did she?'

'Has it been suggested she did?' Tal asked.

The old man shook his head. 'No. But that's the point, isn't it? If she wasn't going down there in the dark for a bit of slap and tickle, what was she going down there for anyway?'

'Willy Thatch could have forced her down there.'

Dai Ponies snorted like one of the horses he had known years ago. He folded his skinny arms across his chest and scowled his disapproval of the inanity of Tal's suggestion. But he said no more, and after a moment Tal turned back, dried his hands on the towel. Casually, in an off-hand tone that did nothing to fool Dai Ponies, he asked, 'Did you say you'd seen her up on the mountain?'

Dai Ponies grinned evilly. 'Seen them all, one time or another. Times have changed a bit just recent, but in the old days it was

184

always the same. Summer evenings, Saturdays, best time. All those young lads takin' their girls to the pictures. Fine night, obvious, but all those boys with raincoats over their arms. Not worried about the weather, though – just grass stains. After the pictures, all goin' grassin', see.'

'And you saw Barbara Porelli going ... grassing?'

'Oh, aye, a few years back now, mind. She'd be still at school then, I suppose, and that's why I paid special attention, like. I mean, recognized she was old Pot-Shot Porelli's daughter – good snooker player, he was – and I guessed there'd be trouble if he found out she was wrigglin' her legs in the air among the ferns back of Pentre pit. Fine summer, that was; she came up every night for a week, as I remember, and you could see miles, you know, clear air? I used to go up by the newt pond at the foot of the tip and look down the hill and you could see them both, strugglin' away like they was in a hell of a hurry. Maybe he was. She didn't care, though – older than her, he was, and kept lookin' about, but she didn't care.'

Tal stared at Dai and there was something in his face that made the old man freeze.

'She was with an older man? A *married*

man, Dai?'

When the steam forced its way out of the kettle spout Tal used a little hot water to warm the pot, threw it away, then made the tea. He heard a step behind him but did not turn. After a moment Lyn spoke.

'I sent the receptionist home, Tal. She's got the sniffs. Better in her bed than passing her cold on to patients in the surgery. You made the tea? I'm dying for a cup. Finished my list, but Evan won't be through for maybe another ten minutes.'

She went into the sitting-room ahead of him. Tal carried the tea-tray in, then had to return to the kitchen for the cups.

'Absent-minded professor,' Lyn said when he came back into the sitting-room, but though there was a half smile on her lips her eyes were watchful. 'Something on your mind?'

Tal shrugged vaguely. Lyn poured the tea, and handed him a cup. She waited expectantly. Tal sipped his tea and frowned.

'Dai Ponies was in.'

'What's wrong with him? He hasn't been down to see you in a hell of a time.'

'Bronchitis.' When Lyn clucked her tongue, Tal nodded. 'I know ... I told him he ought to be at Penceiber. I made it clear that in my view he just won't last out the winter up there. But he did say he'd move to a drier place. God knows where.'

'A barn on the Bwylch farm?'

'Maybe. Up to him… Had a chat with him.'

Lyn raised an eyebrow. 'A gossip, I expect you mean.'

'Something like that. I had the satisfaction of learning, at least, that the acknowledged gossip expert of the mountain doesn't go much on the Mal Powers rumours that Evan's been putting about. Not *valley* rumours, he says, so discounts them entirely.'

Lyn laughed. 'Parochial or nothing.'

'He also said a few things that raised other questions in my mind,' Tal said quietly.

Lyn's smile faded and the laughter in her eyes flickered out like a lamp turning down. 'You're not going to tell me you discussed the murder, and Willy Thatch, with him?'

'Lyn–'

'You've got to leave it, Tal. It's becoming obsessional. I can accept that you were upset. I know that you blame yourself in some stupid way, but you have to snap out of it. It's finished, it's over–'

'No.'

'Tal, it's *over.*'

'Not for me.' As Lyn made a gesture of impatience and turned her face away, Tal put out a hand and touched her arm. 'Please, hear me out. There's been some half-formed arguments at the back of my mind that I've not been able to seize on; they've been there, I've been reaching for them, but a few things Dai Ponies said today started them out into the open for me. First of all, what the hell was Barbara Porelli doing at the Patch, anyway?'

'Now, Tal...' Bewilderment and doubt blurred Lyn's eyes as the question broke through the barrier of irritation she had erected. 'What do you mean?'

'Why did she go to the Patch? Look, consider the story Jack Arthur is raising. For no reason that's been given or explained, Barbara Porelli was walking into the Patch that night. According to the police, Willy Thatch saw her as he came out the Alex and followed her, tried to rape her, strangled her and stole her money. But what the hell was she doing there, anyway?'

Lyn considered the question for a moment. A frown appeared between her eyebrows. 'Did the police say that? Or was it that she was walking past the Patch, and Willy Thatch grabbed her there at the entrance to the lane, forced her down there, and then attacked her?'

'That isn't what the police said,' Tal insisted. 'Moreover, if he had manhandled her down the lane, wouldn't she have been yelling blue murder? How would Willy have coped with that? Hand over her mouth? She'd have bitten him. Only marks were on his face, though. Besides, there were no signs of a struggle in the lane, as far as I know – Adams the Rag made no mention of it, at least, nor Jack Arthur.'

'We can't be sure–'

'All right. I'll grant you it, as a hypothesis. He grabbed her as she passed the lane. Where was she going, then?'

'How the hell should I know?' Lyn replied, nettled.

'Nothing down that road for Barbara Porelli, surely? No friends we know of. No family. Nearest bus stop was a hundred yards the other way. She wasn't going to a pub, not alone, not in the valley! So where was she going? Must have been to meet someone.'

'Now, Tal, I don't see–'

'Let me put it to you, Lyn. Please. It makes no real difference whether we conclude she was walking into the Patch or past it when Willy Thatch attacked her. The fact was, she

must have been in that area to meet someone. Think back, and don't get all angry with
me! When she came to see me here she said
she was going to sort things out herself. Next
thing, she's dead on the Patch. What if she
was going down there to "sort things out"
with her lover?'

Lyn's mouth was set, her lips compressed.
She shook her head. 'What difference does
it make? Willy Thatch killed her.'

'So the police say.'

'As does the evidence.'

'I cannot accept deliberate murder on the
part of Willy. But even at its worst, I think
we ought to know why she was down there
– because, believe me, Lyn, she *must* have
been *on* the Patch when Willy attacked her.'

'You accept he did attack her, then!'

'That's incontrovertible.'

'Then why–' Lyn raised a hand and
slapped the arm of her chair.

'*Think*, Lyn! Assume she was going to the
Patch to meet a man. *He could have been
there when Willy Thatch attacked her!*'

Lyn stared at him uncomprehendingly for
a long moment. Then she frowned. 'He
couldn't have been. He'd have intervened.'

'Would he?'

'Of course he–' The words died away. She

chewed thoughtfully at her lower lip, then shook her head. 'It's not on, Tal. You're suggesting–'

'I'm suggesting she went on the Patch to meet a man. It's more than likely he would be there before her – she wouldn't have wanted to wait on waste ground alone, after dark. If he was, he'd have seen Willy Thatch attack her, and he did nothing to save her life.'

Lyn shuddered slightly, as though she were touched by a cold hand. Her eyes were very wide.

'Why would he do that?'

Tal spread out his fingers, stared at them, fingertips still wrinkled a little from the warm water in which he had washed after surgery.

'I talked to Dai Ponies, as I told you. He rambles a bit. But he did tell me he remembered Barbara Porelli. There's one thing you can say about Dai: he's old, but he's got a long memory for the young girls and their boys on the mountain.'

'He saw her up there?'

'Oh, not recently. Some years ago. Courting. For a week, or thereabouts, he saw her come up one summer with a man. Just that week. But he watched them; saw what happened. She'd have been at school then.'

'The man–'

'Was older than Barbara. Do you see what I'm getting at now?'

He guessed she did, but she did not want to reply. She wanted him to say it. He sipped his tea, considering.

'Barbara Porelli told me she needed money and could get it – *from a man who could afford it*. She had a lover, years ago, here in the valley. An older man. Now what if it hadn't ended then? What if he had continued to see her during her wanton years in Cardiff? What if she had come back to the valley not only to get my professional opinion, but also to see her lover, and screw some money out of him? An older man, a man with some money behind him...' He looked directly at Lyn, and grimaced.

'You said Jack Arthur was wrong, earlier,' she said.

'When he said we should be looking for a married man as Barbara's lover? Yes, well, it would seem the inspector maybe wasn't so far out after all. Maybe the man who was waiting for Barbara on the Patch had a marriage to lose, and that's why he let Willy Thatch go ahead and strangle the girl.'

Lyn's face was stiff. 'He wouldn't necessarily *have* to be married. He could have been fearful of losing something else.'

'Like what?'

'Status,' she said hurriedly as Evan Ritchie came into the room.

2

Legislation passed by distant Parliaments had little or no effect upon the Conservative Club. Changes in the licensing laws and Sunday opening had not drawn the club's clientele away to the public houses; the legalization of betting shop might have ended the reign of the bookie's 'runner' in many streets but not in the club – he remained ensconced in the billiards room with his time-clock, his tin money-box and his pile of betting slips and receipts, like an Eastern potentate receiving homage and dispensing favours, only more loved.

The basic reason why the club remained inviolate was simply that it was regarded as a family club. The word 'family' was a mis-nomer essentially, since women and children were barred from the premises except on particular 'social' evenings, but it was true that there was a 'family' of men who had used the club for many years and had formed an attachment for its beer, its billiards room, its dominoes room and its tiny concert room which they passed on to their sons. Social cachet or right-leaning political conviction had nothing to do with membership, of course – a man had to be left-wing in order to get on the club committee – but there were a few middle-class members who openly courted the Conservative cause and even wore blue ribands at General Election time.

Evan Ritchie was one of them.

He sat on the high stool at the lounge bar and ordered a gin for himself, a whisky for Tal. There were very few people in the room; bursts of laughter from the concert room announced that the club members, having sampled and enjoyed a comedy turn a few weeks earlier, had now re-engaged the comedian for a social evening to which wives were invited. In a little while they would come flooding out of the room for refreshment – the single men into the bar, and married men with their wives into the lounge. It was all, Tal considered, quite ritualistic.

'I didn't want to talk in front of Lyn,' Evan Ritchie said, handing the whisky glass to Tal, 'because I felt a bit … uncomfortable.'

'I don't see why you need to feel that way. The decision has been taken, Lyn's packing it in, and there's no rancour as far as I know.'

'It's not that,' Ritchie replied. 'Things have … changed. I think maybe you and Lyn might … reconsider the position.'

Slowly Tal reached for the soda siphon and aimed a brief, deliberate splash of soda into his drink. He watched the effervescence subside and then in a quiet voice he said, 'I think you'd better explain yourself, Evan. The decision *has* been taken, after all.'

'Oh, now, let's be clear,' Ritchie said hastily. 'I'm not going back on what I said about Lyn and the abortion issue. She was wrong, you'll agree on that, and I stick by what I said. But … well, the fact is, it may be you'll feel it's no longer necessary that she should leave the practice.'

'Why?'

Ritchie's handsome face displayed a marked earnestness; it was the kind of sincerity he showed on a public platform and Tal distrusted it now as he did then. He picked up his glass and toyed with it as Evan spoke.

'It seems to me that since I was the one who was making an issue of the abortion decision, when you were prepared to let it slide, it should be me who should go. After all, you and Lyn see eye to eye on many things where I differ with you. It's a bit silly that Lyn should be the one to leave the practice. Let's face facts, Tal: if she goes, and I stay, the result could be that our own working relationship could worsen. You might feel a certain resentment... Anyway, I've been thinking about it, and I reckon it would be better for all of us if I went, and Lyn stayed.'

Tal sipped at his whisky and soda. 'Do you have another practice in mind?'

Ritchie hesitated. 'I think I could slot in over in Abercrwys, with Frederick.'

Tal put down his glass and stared at it. Coolly he said, 'I hear that Talman had a heart attack a few weeks back.'

'Oh?'

'I suppose that means he won't be standing for Abercrwys again.'

'I ... I wouldn't know.'

'Oh, come on, Evan,' Tal said snappishly. 'Don't be so bloody coy. Why can't you come out and say what you really mean? You're not concerned about Lyn and me, or about any future professional relationship you and I might have. Talman's illness means he won't stand again; that would leave you in with a chance to take his place, if you were working in Abercrwys – and the recent mileage you've got locally from the Hospital Action Committee campaign means you'd stand a good chance.'

'I don't discount that, of course,' Ritchie said in a voice as stiff as his face, 'but the other reasons I mentioned–'

'They're irrelevant, Evan. I told you long ago, don't seek excuses. Have the courage to go for what you want boldly, and don't rationalize when it's not necessary. Be honest, for God's sake!'

Ritchie was rattled and angry. 'Like *you* are, I suppose! Go for things boldly! You're a fine one to talk. Burying yourself in this valley, with the kind of brain you have! You threw away all the best chances for a life between these narrow bloody hills, and even now *you* tell *me* to be honest when you're not even honest yourself! What about Lyn, for instance? You've kept her dangling for years. Why aren't you honest about her? Why don't you marry her, for God's sake – instead of telling me where my weaknesses lie?'

The politician in Evan Ritchie caught up with the inner man, and he stopped abruptly, took a deep breath, and a drink. When he spoke again he was calmer. 'Anyway, think it over, Tal. I've decided to go to Abercrwys. That means Lyn needn't leave the partnership. You and she can carry on without me. Things might even be happier for everyone. I never really fitted in with you two, anyway.'

He finished his drink and stalked away without another word.

It was all very well for Evan Ritchie to say he was going and Lyn could stay. Tal knew the answer to that one already: the watershed had been reached, and Lyn had made a decision. Evan Ritchie's leaving would make no difference – she would be leaving the valley. As for Evan himself, Tal could now see some light in the murk surrounding his partner's recent conduct. The smear campaign over Mal Powers had been closely calculated; when Dai Ponies had said it wasn't just valley gossip he had been right – the malice and motivation had been deeper. Evan must have heard that the Abercrwys candidature could be his for the asking, and he had set the seal on it by making a public showing here in the valley, before he made his move to Abercrwys and a political rather than a medical life. It all began to fit, and if Mal Powers suffered be-cause of it Evan would weep no tears. He was unscrupulous and hard and would make a successful politician. If Mal Powers went down the political drain at the council meet-ing later in the week, that would do no harm to Evan. He was set fair – he would have the position and status he really wanted...

Status... What had Lyn meant by that remark? Tal had had no opportunity to question her once Evan had entered the room. Tal guessed that what she had been trying to say was that marriage wasn't necessarily the thing that might have had to be protected by Barbara Porelli's lover. It could have been status – the sort of status that a man could lose if a scandal broke. Political status, for one thing. What was it Evan Ritchie had been doing the night Barbara Porelli died? He had left Tal and Lyn with Ieuan James while he went off to attend the Midgely case, but he must have been late getting back home. The police had tried the surgery, then when there was no answer there they had rung through to Lyn Morgan and called Tal out. But Evan–

The doors of the concert room opened. The first trickle of people came hurrying out to slake a thirst sharpened by laughter. Half-a-dozen men and women headed for Tal's bar, but one young man walked in a different direction, towards the main bar on the other side of the corridor.

It was Colin Owen.

Tal stared at his retreating figure. He had been thinking of the man who might have been Barbara Porelli's lover, and Colin

Owen had appeared. He hesitated for a moment, then as people bustled around him he picked up his drink, left the room and made his way across the corridor.

He stood just inside the door for a moment. Colin Owen was at the bar, getting himself a drink. He seemed to be alone. Tal waited to make sure. The young man took his glass of beer and headed for a seat in the far corner of the room. He sat there alone. He stared at his beer despondently, as though he doubted whether happiness lay in its depths.

Slowly Tal walked across the room.

When he stood immediately in front of Colin Owen's table there was a short pause and then Owen looked up. Surprise flared in his eyes, then it was replaced by swift embarrassment.

'Dr ... Dr Rees!'

'Colin,' Tal acknowledged gravely, and slid into a seat beside the young man. 'Good comedian?'

Perhaps there was something in his tone that suggested he saw it as odd that Colin Owen should be watching a comedian in the Conservative Club when the girl he had loved was not long in her grave. If so, it might have accounted for the air of nonchalance that Colin Owen struggled to affect. 'Not bad,' he said. 'Seen worse. Not really my style, though. Dad insisted I came along. He's a member, see; saw this comic a few weeks back, so thought I'd enjoy it.' He managed a weak smile. 'Got to humour the older generation, you know, from time to time. Dad's with his own butties now, though, so I escaped in here for a drink.'

'With me. Reluctantly.'

Colin Owen did not look at Tal, but his hand shook slightly as he reached out, picked up his glass and took a long drink of beer.

'Don't know why you should say that, Dr Rees.'

'I embarrass you.'

'Not at all.' His failure to look at Tal belied his words, nevertheless. 'Why should I feel uneasy in your presence?'

'Because you're afraid I'll start talking to you about Barbara Porelli.'

Colin Owen leaned back in his chair. He looked around the room, and a small sigh escaped his lips. It sounded like relief. He took a deep breath and turned his head to look squarely at Tal. He injected confidence into his eyes, and a studied carelessness into the set of his mouth. More; when he spoke, it was with a ring of callousness. It was as though he had been waiting to see Tal to tell him; to convince him of the truth of his own feelings.

'Barbara Porelli is *dead*, Dr Rees.'

He meant more than that; practising the words in front of the mirror, he had tested the nuance, emphasized the hidden yet forceful meaning. Tal grimaced.

'She was dead when last we met.'

'But it's all over now. Finished. Her murderer is dead, she is dead, and whatever I felt for her is dead too. I was stupid, you know that? I never really saw her clearly, I think. She was like a drug with me, for a while – I even wanted to marry her! Imagine that – an easy lay like Barbara Porelli. I mean, half the businessmen in Cardiff had got across her from what she told me, and I was prepared to marry her! And she said she was turning me down. *Me!* I tell you, she was like a drug, but I kicked the habit. Sat down and thought about it after I saw you. That's all it took. Now it's finished. And I can live again.'

'No sense of responsibility?'

'For what?'

Tal saw the defiant challenge in the young man's eyes, and sighed. 'She *was* pregnant, Colin.'

'That wasn't why she died!'

'No?'

Owen frowned, puzzled. 'What do you mean?'

Tal countered with another question. 'When she phoned you, did you arrange to meet her – the night she died?'

Owen shook his head, brushed the hair from his eyes. 'No. She told me she didn't want us to meet again. I came up to the valley that day, stayed with Dad, went for a long walk that evening to try to blow cobwebs from my mind, but I didn't arrange to see Barbara.'

'And you didn't see her?'

'I just said... Now hold on. What's this about? No, I didn't see her, but that bloody maniac Willy Thatch did and hanged himself as a result. And it's over.'

But you're not off the emotional hook yet, Tal thought, whatever you might proclaim. I can see the panicked hurt in your eyes, the fear that you can't control the agonies you have – and deny – inside you. But he didn't say it. Instead, Tal said, 'She was meeting someone, Colin.'

The stress he laid on the words brought home his meaning. Colin Owen stared at him with a glazed anger in his eyes. 'That's rubbish.'

'She told me at the surgery she was going

203

to sort things out with a man who could afford to pay her money. You?'

'No. I told you–'

'Then who?'

Owen's eyelids dropped as though he sought to conceal from Tal the thoughts that were present in his mind. He sat rigidly in his chair, thinking hard. Slowly he shook his head. 'I can't think there was anyone she would want to see up here.'

'There was no other man, the same time as you?'

'No!' The word flashed out, righteous anger underscored with doubt.

'Then who came before you?'

He did not answer. Tal knew that Colin Owen would probably be unable to answer and too proud to admit it. There had been many lovers before him; names would have been something Barbara would probably have withheld. That way lay pain. Numbers, yes; names, no.

'She was a funny girl,' Colin Owen muttered, seeking a way through the thicket of doubt and pain by memories. 'She was bright, you know that? There I was, higher degree, doing research, but she was quicker with figures than me, you know. She had eight O-levels at school, and only left because of an argument about uniform. If she'd stayed in the sixth she'd have ended up at university, easy. Too bloody independent, she was.'

He shook his head, snorted, smiled faintly as warmer memories returned.

'But she was stupid too, really. Independence was so bloody important to her, breaking away from her family and their way of looking at things was all so necessary for her. When she went down to Cardiff first she was sensible enough, having refused a university chance, to get herself in with a firm of bloody accountants. She *worked* for two years, you know; worked bloody hard, got her Part I Accountancy examinations, got started on the rest. And then dropped the lot. Know why? Because her mother told her that her father approved! She didn't *want* her old man's approval, so she threw the lot, took a secretarial course, started doing temp work and drifted around the firms for a while. But she was still sharp over figures and accounts – and she could show me a thing or two.'

Talking about her was a form of release for him suddenly; he had denied her a few minutes earlier, but now it was almost as though he had forgotten Tal was with him. He needed an audience while he talked about

Barbara Porelli, and it could have been anyone. He just wanted to talk.

'She was a hell of a lot of fun, and she knew how to enjoy herself, and she could say things to you that would make your hair curl, but it was all surface stuff, you know? Out to shock, I suppose, kick over the traces, but all the men she met, that was the kind of girl they wanted, and she gave it to them. But not with me. It was different with me. To start with, when I met her again some years after we'd known each other in the valleys, I needed help – not the kind she'd given all those fly-by-nights around Bute Street, but real help.'

He grinned at the thought. 'Me, a graduate in physics, doing a master's in business administration, and I turned for help to a girl who left school at sixteen! But that's the way things turn out, isn't it? Educated to the eyebrows, and good for bugger all!'

He turned his thoughts inward for a little while, his eyes lowered, perhaps beginning to feel sorrow for himself rather than sadness for what he had lost with Barbara. Tal brought him back.

'How exactly did she help you?'

Colin Owen scratched his head, took another drink. 'I was doing a research project on the administration of medium-size companies. I'd spent time with three in Cardiff and then got a placement in this company in Elgar Street. Who should be there but Barbara, working as a private sec. We got chatting, of course, about the valley, and I took her out, we had a bit of a time – and then she found me poring over some of the books in the company. And she resolved the problem. Oh, I was okay on line of command, management techniques, computer services and all that jazz, but she was able to point out to me the essential management problem in this particular company. Nothing more and nothing less than cash flow. Didn't put it in my reports, of course, because it was confidential, and strictly none of my business. But it helped my understanding of the whole business problem. And it was Barbara who pointed it all out to me. She had an accountant's eye, that girl, and she spotted the whole thing for me. Very simple, of course, but weighed against the background at that time, all too clear – if you knew what to look for.'

'And she knew.'

'That's it.' Owen now began to speak with the commitment of an academic to his subject, almost forgetting they were talking about Barbara Porelli, not a set of accounts. 'You've got to see it against a whole background of business, of course. It was a medium-sized company, with a network of contacts throughout South Wales – built up, I've no doubt, on the sort of back-handers to local government officials and minor works contractors that is prevalent throughout the industry – but it was a solid enough concern for years. Then it came up with a brilliant new idea about ten years ago, pumped a lot of money into it, developed a new product, and started selling hard. But the problem was, really, it sold too hard. And then, just as its lines were really extended, there was a financial squeeze, we entered an economic recession, all sorts of people were going to the wall – architects, building contractors, supplies merchants – and cash became a real problem. All companies like to exist on credit; the banks lend on long-term gains; but workmen need paying *now* and so a cash flow problem builds up. Bills don't get paid, interest charges rocket, sub-contractors go bankrupt, the whole industry goes into recession and collapses.'

'This firm collapsed?'

Owen shook his head. 'No. It pulled through, in fact. God knows how, but it managed to keep its head above water. I was surprised, mind; the way Barbara showed me the figures she'd calculated I thought it was odds-on they'd go to the wall. Anyway … as I say, she should have stayed in the accountancy field. She'd have done well…'

He finished his drink moodily. He looked up, glanced around the bar, and grimaced. 'Instead of which, she's gone. And *he's* all right.'

Tal looked up, followed the line of Colin Owen's nod. Standing near the bar, edged with sycophantic drinkers, was a man in a brown suit. He had broad, powerful shoulders that suggested he had swung more than a few picks in his time, but his stubby fingers held a double gin and tonic as though they had been born to the good life. He wore his hair fashionably long and his skin was tanned. He stood, grinning and chatting, with his legs braced apart as though he were standing on a quarterdeck, but the woman who stood a carefully measured two feet away from him and wore a false smile at his jokes cared little for the company and less for him. Her blonde hair, carefully set, proclaimed her age; her presence proclaimed her ownership of the man; her eyes proclaimed her dislike of him. It was a well-known fact they rarely spoke to each other, except in company.

Tal turned a puzzled face to Colin Owen.

'Tommy Elias? What's he got to do with it?'

Colin Owen stood up and grunted. 'It was his firm Barbara was working for in Cardiff. Want another drink?'

3

Lyn Morgan folded her arms and glared at Tal with her most efficient doctor-patient glare. She was displeased.

'If you want my opinion, you'd be well advised to drop it.'

'I could go to the police,' Tal suggested, none too enthusiastically.

'You'd get blown out of the door on a gale of laughter,' Lyn announced angrily. 'Do you want to make a complete fool of yourself, Tal?'

Tal set his mouth stubbornly. 'I think certain questions are raised–'

'Questions, my backside! Wild theories, that's how I'd describe the whole thing! Look, Tal, face facts. Willy Thatch followed that girl into the Patch, tried to rape her, then murdered her. Shattered by what he had done, when he was called upon to face the music he committed suicide. Now that's where it all ends – for the police, and for me. It ought to end there for you, too.'

'The police won't re-open the matter because they are simply concerned with their own internal inquiry over the suicide.'

'That doesn't matter, damn it! To all intents and purposes it is closed. Oh, I know you're full of all sorts of twisted guilts about the part you played in it all – you feel you should have gone to see Willy Thatch as you promised, you think that you must bear some sort of responsibility for all that's happened. All right; but that doesn't mean you should set yourself up as an amateur detective and start poking around in other people's lives, perhaps distressing them unduly–'

'Tommy Elias hasn't got on with his wife for years,' Tal insisted stubbornly.

'It doesn't follow logically from that, surely, that it was Elias whom Barbara had arranged to meet?'

'Dai Ponies could tell me who it was she used to court on the mountain; if it was Tommy Elias–'

'Dai *Ponies!* Gossip on the hills, wriggling in the ferns – that's about all you've got to go on, isn't it, Tal? Can't you see how stupid it all is? Anyway, I gather you've already tried to see the old man.'

Tal nodded unhappily. 'Aye, well, he wasn't very communicative the other day at the surgery when I pressed him about it; if you wait and listen to Dai he'll tell you a lot of gossip, but *ask* him and he clams up. I made the mistake of asking him then. I'd play him more carefully now, if I could find him.'

'He's not living at the pit, then?'

Tal shook his head. 'No, the few possessions he owns have been removed. I told him he needed to find somewhere warmer and drier, but I've no idea where he might have gone.'

'Well, I think you should leave him – and this nonsense – alone. You're a damn good doctor, Tal; it's a bit late in life to start thinking about turning detective. What do you know about digging for dirt, anyway?'

Nothing, Tal thought to himself, but he knew someone who did.

The office was tastelessly elegant. It was set in an office block, newly built on the outskirts of Penarth, and it held two streamlined filing systems suspended against the wall, functional and expensive light controls, a long, curved desk that shone, and a deep-pile carpet that raised all sorts of static against

Tal's shoes. He was alone in the room, and though there was the intermittent chatter of a typewriter from the room beyond he had seen no sign of any staff since Ieuan James had ushered him into the office and then gone out again, apologizing, with the remark that he'd be back in a few minutes. Perhaps the office was designed so that clients should not see the staff, however; modern business practice involved setting people at ease, ensuring that the client felt he was getting a personal attention, and was not simply caught up in the maw of an impersonal machine.

Tal walked across to the window and looked out at a vista that covered most of the Penarth seafront; strangely enough, he thought of Evan Ritchie. Ieuan James lived and moved in the sort of circles that Evan wanted and hankered after: Evan wanted the golf club in Penarth, not at Trefowydd, the yacht club at Rhoose, not the Conservative Club in Treharne; holidays in Cannes, not stories of trips to Barry Island. He might get it yet, if he made it politically, and could perhaps become a power in the land before he ended up in one of Ieuan James's creations displayed on the wall.

Tal squinted at the drawing framed with gilt and black; it was dated 1962, and showed a massive crematorium complex designed for a mid-west brotherhood in the United States. Returning ten per cent of their income into the brotherhood, they could afford to shell out thousands of dollars for such an ugly project, Tal supposed.

'Awful, isn't it?'

Tal started, turned, and saw Ieuan James coming back into the room with a sheaf of papers in his hand. He tossed them on to the desk, apologized for keeping Tal waiting and explained that paperwork was anathema to him but ruled his life.

'That design, though–' he nodded towards the wall 'started me on an illustrious career in the States which came to an abrupt end. I can laugh about it now, but it was rough at the time.'

'What happened?' Tal asked, taking the deep leather seat to which James gestured.

'Well, I suppose I have to admit I over-stretched myself,' James smiled, 'and there are plenty who'll tell you that, anyway. You see, after I won a couple of awards in 1957 and branched out with crematoria designs in '58, I thought I'd try my hand in the States. An American exhibition in 1960, a couple of companies formed in 1962 and things were going well. And then ... well, I learned things were a damn sight worse in the States than ever they were in Wales.'

'How do you mean?'

James waved a hand that took in the scene outside his windows. 'They'll tell you that the business world in the vale means *dealing* with people behind the counter, you know? There's a bit of that, sure; but in the States, hell, it's rife! The fact is, I didn't go about greasing enough palms and then a commission pinned me like a butterfly. Others who had paid out the right sort of cash got away with it, but me – I got keelhauled over certain fire-resistant materials I'd used in a high-level project. It killed my companies. So, bruised and battered but wiser, I came back home.'

Tal glanced around the elegant office, took in the gold-embossed wallpaper. 'You've done well enough since your return.'

'Success is relative,' James replied modestly, 'but, well, yes, I've done pretty well. And still am. Once I'm clear on the hospital project in the valley I'm into a civil building design in the Midlands – it's all work, believe me.'

He sounded as though he wanted to impress Tal; it left Tal with a curious feeling of uneasiness. The trappings of success were around him, he felt out of his depth, and it wasn't necessary for James to stress his business acumen.

'Anyway,' James continued, 'you're not here to talk about my career. I imagine you want to discuss the campaign over the hospital. I know you've been uneasy about it but—'

'No. It's not that I want to discuss.'

James raised his eyebrows. 'Oh? I'm sorry. All right, fire away.'

'Well, I suppose it is connected with the hospital campaign, really,' Tal said lamely, reluctant suddenly to expose himself to the same kind of criticism that had come from Lyn. 'I mean … well, your sources of information about Mal Powers…'

Ieuan James's eyes became watchful. He placed one hand against his jawline; the slender fingers moved up to caress lightly the lobe of his ear. He pulled at it, like a dog pulling at a recalcitrant bone.

'I'll be frank, Dr Rees. I gather from Evan Ritchie that you're not happy about the fact I did some digging. In view of that, I'm reluctant to supply you with the names of my informants—'

'You misread the situation. I don't want their names in order to argue with them or with you. I want to use them, if they are suitable people.'

216

'*Use* them?' The hand fell away; James leaned forward with his elbow on the desk. 'What on earth for?'

'To make a few inquiries connected with the death of Barbara Porelli.'

To his credit, Ieuan James's features did not change. He remained completely unmoved, betrayed no surprise, no shock. But he could not keep the interest out of his voice.

'What sort of inquiries do you have in mind?'

'If these people are of the kind who–'

'Take it from me,' James forestalled him. 'They're efficient and trustworthy. One's a journalist. The other involved in the Powers investigation is a building contractor and won't fit, but I know a man in Cardiff who can do a sniffing job for you – if you tell me the kind of thing you have in mind.'

'Tommy Elias, principally.'

This time, James's face did move. His forehead became corrugated with swift, thoughtful calculation; his eyes flickered, something moving in them, deep, a shadow passing over water. He smiled mirthlessly.

'My friend from the *Confrontation* programme,' he said. 'But what's his connection with that girl?'

Tal explained swiftly. Barbara Porelli had

worked in Cardiff for Tommy Elias. What if they had known each other in the valley years before? What if they had remained lovers? What if she had arranged to see Elias at the Patch, to get some money from him, the night she died?

'I don't understand,' James said slowly. 'Why would she think she could get money from him?'

'What I do know is that he wasn't the father of the child she was carrying,' Tal replied. 'But maybe she wanted some sort of revenge on Elias. It's possible he had been her lover – maybe her seducer – those years ago on the mountain. It's possible when he gave her the job in Cardiff it was with a view to having her again. But there might have been another reason why he would have agreed to meet her at the Patch.'

'You haven't given me *one* reason yet.'

'His marriage. He might have wanted to keep the story of a liaison with Barbara from his wife.'

'I understand he and his wife barely speak to each other.'

'That still doesn't mean she couldn't make life uncomfortable for him if she had learned of an affair in Cardiff,' Tal insisted. 'But there is another reason, as I said. A

218

business reason.'

A flicker of interest moved in James's face; he was moving to more familiar ground.

'A business reason?'

'Tommy Elias was in financial trouble. The recession in the building industry came at a time when he was just establishing his industrial operations – you know, selling those briquettes from the slack he pumps from old pit heaps. He had a cash flow problem – and Barbara Porelli knew about it.'

'I don't see–'

'Neither do I, at this stage. It's what I want you and your people to try to find out for me. The thing is this: look at the string of events. Barbara Porelli discovers Tommy Elias is in financial trouble; she becomes pregnant and returns to the valley; she dies. I want to know if there is any possible connection.'

'The girl was killed by a chap called Jones, surely?'

'Willy Thatch. So the police say. But if she *was* meeting Elias, he might have been at the Patch. Why didn't he stop the attack? That's what I want to know. And the first thing to find out is whether or not Elias gave Barbara a job in his company on account of philanthropy or lust.'

James smiled thinly. 'You have a succinct

way of putting things, Dr Rees. And it all sounds very thin and nebulous to me, as a case. But … well, I'll tell you. The first time I ever met Tommy Elias was in that TV programme, *Confrontation*. He gave me a right going-over, that time. I'm enough of a dirty fighter, and sufficiently vengeful to be prepared to help you. All right, Dr Rees, leave it with me. If there's any dirt on Elias, I'll dig it out. And if there's any connection between him and the girl – I'll find it.' He stood up, extended his hand. His grip was firm. 'I'll be in touch. Okay?'

CHAPTER V

The days slipped past and Tal was in his usual routine: lines of men waiting for their 'doctor's paper', anxious mothers-to-be, coughs and colds, ear infections and cut knees, impetigo, measles and mumps. He saw little of Evan Ritchie and not much of Lyn. It was not that she was avoiding him so much as the fact that her work seemed to be taking her out around the streets more, and she did not stop for a cup of tea with him after surgery hours.

Until Friday.

She came into his sitting-room with the evening newspaper which had just been delivered through the letter box. She had already unfolded it and re-folded it to high-light the front page for Tal.

'Well, there it is, then,' she said in an angry tone.

The banner headline was thick and black: TRIUMPH FOR ENVIRONMENTAL GROUPS. Tal glanced up at Lyn and frowned.

'What's this?' he asked.

'This afternoon's planning committee meeting,' she replied. 'You'd better read it.'

Quickly, Tal scanned the columns.

An astonishing reversal of fortunes for opponents of the Llandarog Hospital scheme was brought about at the planning meeting this afternoon. The majority, led by Maldwyn Powers, had succeeded in scotching the hospital building programme in favour of the Pont Newydd Road scheme at the last meeting, but today the majority melted when a motion was raised to reverse the earlier decision. With only three voting against and two abstain-ing, the motion was carried. It was a remarkable overturning of a previously solid position, and can only be attributed to the campaign which has been effectively waged under the leadership of Dr Evan Ritchie. Mr Powers was not available for comment afterwards, but it has been announced that he has resigned both from the planning committee and the main council, presumably on the ground that today's vote is to be seen as one of no confidence in his leadership.

The events of this afternoon must be seen as a triumph for the environmental groups who have worked so hard to preserve all that is fine in the valley heritage. The planning committee decision, which effectively means that the signing of contracts for the hospital project can now go ahead, follows hard on the heels of the successful plea made by the Cwmdare Trust to obtain compensation from Elias Industries Ltd for the acquisition of the cottages on the north slope...

Lyn sat down in the chair facing Tal and scowled.

'Take a look inside,' she said.

Tal opened the paper. The leading article on the inside page was a briefly worded and hurriedly assembled appreciation of the hard work Maldwyn Powers had undertaken over the years for the benefit of the valley community. On the facing page was a photograph of Evan Ritchie, with the caption: *Dr Evan*

Ritchie, leader of the Hospital Action Committee, who will shortly be taking up a new post in Abercrwys.

Tal stared at the picture sourly. It was a good likeness, displaying all the confidence and good looks that Evan could show to the camera.

'Did you know Evan was contemplating leaving the partnership?' Lyn asked.

'He told me the other night at the club.'

'Politics? Talman's place?'

'That's about it.'

'You didn't tell me,' Lyn said quietly.

'I didn't think it would make any difference,' Tal replied.

There was a short silence. 'No,' Lyn said heavily, 'I don't suppose it does.'

Tal looked back to the article on Maldwyn Powers. A slow anger stirred in his veins. 'Evan shouldn't have done this. We could have won without stirring mud around Mal Powers. There's nothing to say he resigned because of allegations made, but it's perfectly obvious why the rest of the committee changed their minds. They were pressured into it, scared of being painted with the same brush. It's a shame – Powers gave a lot to this community. It's all wrong that he should resign under this kind of scurrilous

223

rumour that Evan's been putting about.'

'And for which, as yet, not one atom of proof has been produced.'

Tal nodded. 'Mal Powers must have something to be ashamed of, or he wouldn't have given up this way. But it's a bad way for a man to go.'

'The rumour is that he took a handout of three hundred pounds a few years back, in connection with the swimming pool at Tynewydd. It seems little enough to hang a man with.'

Tal sighed. There was sadness in his chest that lay there like a physical weight. Evan's campaign left a nasty taste in his mouth: he would have wished they could have fought this battle cleanly, or not at all. But it was over now, finished. The road scheme would have to be sent back to its original routing, the contracts for the Llandarog Hospital could be placed, tenders accepted, commissioned designs paid for. It was just a pity that it all couldn't have been achieved in some other way, at the end.

'And what about you, Tal?'

'Me?'

She was looking at him quizzically, with an odd turn to her lip. 'Your detective work,' she said.

He frowned. 'I've heard nothing as yet.'

'Let's hope that Ieuan James's informants come up with something more positive, and *cleaner*, than they did over Maldwyn Powers,' she said, almost sneering.

'It's a different kind of issue, Lyn.'

'Does that mean you don't mind this time if James comes up with dirt you can't prove?'

The anger that had been stirring in Tal now flared; perhaps it was fanned by a certain degree of guilt he felt at having approached James at all, perhaps it was simply that he needed an outlet – any outlet – for emotions stirred over Maldwyn Powers's resignation.

'You're confusing issues, Lyn! I certainly do not approve of what's happened over Mal Powers, but let's be quite clear about what I'm trying to do! The police are turning a blind eye to what happened at the Patch that night. I keep thinking about it all, every night. We keep assuming the facts are as Jack Arthur said, and I've raised another hypothesis. But, you know, maybe I've not gone far enough.'

'You've gone too far for me, Tal.'

'That's because you're not prepared to question and dig into something unpleasant! But I keep turning over in my mind what Adams the Rag told me at the forensic laboratory shortly after Barbara Porelli was killed. We were interrupted by Jack Arthur, so I didn't really have the chance to talk to Adams at length about it, but what it comes down to is this. He claimed that there was very little bruising about Barbara's thighs, and though there was a tear in the vaginal wall, and some evidence of rough handling, the kind of evidence he would have expected if she had put up a struggle just wasn't there.'

Lyn frowned and shook her head.

'I don't see what you're getting at. The girl's clothes–'

'Her underclothes were torn, and she had been assaulted. That's easily proved. But what Adams was saying to me was that he wasn't at all clear *when* Barbara had been assaulted.'

'There was blood on Willy Thatch's face, and–'

'I'm sorry, Lyn, but you're missing the point. Look, Jack Arthur's hypothesis is really based upon the following sequence: first, Willy follows Barbara down into the Patch, then attacks her – for sexual satisfaction. She fights, scratches his face, he loses control completely and strangles her. But when does he assault her? Get the facts straight, now. If he assaulted her when she was struggling there'd be evidence of bruising.'

'All right, then, he assaulted her when she was unconscious.'

'From the blow on the head? Or when she was dead from strangulation?'

Lyn's eyes were stony. She did not wish to pursue the conversation but was unable to resist Tal's insistence. But the tone of her voice made her displeasure clear.

'I would guess,' she said icily, 'that he attacked her, she was knocked unconscious, he assaulted her while she lay there, and then when she came round he strangled her.'

'Why didn't he complete the assault – why didn't he rape her?'

'I can't imagine. Maybe he was about to when she regained consciousness and opened her mouth to scream.'

Tal nodded. 'So he killed her. He didn't bother to complete the rape then, just got up, leaving her lying there, picked up her hand-bag, took her money, threw the bag away and walked home, stopping to pick up a bottle on the way at an off-licence. It won't wash, Lyn.'

'Why not?' she demanded.

'First of all, because it's *Willy Thatch* we're talking about! Can you see him behaving like that? I can't. Look, I can imagine him robbing the girl – I can even imagine him trying

227

to have it off with her. But to do what Jack Arthur claims he did ... I just can't see it.'

'The evidence is there.'

'What evidence? Nothing to connect Willy with the assault.'

'The scratches on his face—'

'They prove he *fought* with her. But, you know, Adams mentioned no evidence on her *body*. No semen, no pubic hair, no fibres, nothing to prove it was Willy who tore at her body.'

'But if it wasn't Willy, who was it, for God's sake?'

'Maybe the man she had gone to the Patch to meet.'

Lyn was silent for a moment. Slowly she said, 'That's ridiculous, Tal.'

'Willy could have knocked her down. He could have robbed her. There he is, staggering back to the road. And only then does the man Barbara had come to meet emerge from the shadows – where he had hidden, so as not to be seen with the girl.'

'But he would have gone to her assistance.'

'Not if he'd hoped Willy would kill her.'

Lyn's eyes were round, but she was silent. Tal grimaced.

'You accept all this is possible, then?'

'Possible, but—'

'He could have come out, Lyn, carefully. Willy Thatch was gone – but Barbara was still breathing. He could have crouched over her, put his hands on her neck, strangled her – and *then* torn her clothes to make the assault that much more convincing. And then, when Willy Thatch remembered only vaguely what had happened, and confessed under police suggestions, he was in the clear...'

She was shaking her head. 'I can't accept it, Tal.'

'Because you don't want to, Lyn. I've had it on my mind for days. Ever since I heard she had been working for Tommy Elias–'

'Oh, Tal, you're not suggesting–'

'I'm suggesting nothing yet. All I know is Dai Ponies said she'd been with an older man, and a married man could well have the reason to kill that girl if she was after money as I *know* she was. But the police won't even follow that one up–'

'So you enlist the aid of hired men of Cardiff,' she said contemptuously. 'And why, for God's sake? Not for Willy Thatch, not for his widow, not even for Barbara Porelli. It's for *yourself*, Tal – and that's the worst reason of all. It's stupid, it's dangerously obsessional, it can lead to trouble and unhappiness, and it's egotistical. You're trying to prove that you were wrong and that you can now make up for it. It's the sort of self-centred interest that could kill you, Tal...'

2

Pen-Rhys House was ablaze with lights. Cars were parked along the length of the driveway, some placed on the grass verge, some pulled in under the trees. The light above the open gateway shone wetly on the rhododendron bushes as the rain slanted down and Lyn peered through the windscreen to direct Tal to a small parking area left in front of the garage, right ahead of them.

'It means we can make a quick getaway, at least,' Tal said.

Neither he nor Lyn had really wanted to come tonight. But it would have been churlish, they both agreed, to refuse Evan's invitation – it was by way of a celebration for the activists both on the Hospital Action Committee and the Cwmdare Trust. Evan had invited all who had contributed to the success of the campaign, and, it would seem, he had even persuaded Mr and Mrs Elias to come along. Tal had no doubt that Tommy Elias would see his acceptance of the invitation as his way of cocking a snook at the Cwmdare Trust: pay them off for the danger to the condemned cottages he might, but he was also prepared to face them in public with a bold face.

Lyn extracted an umbrella from under the car seat and struggled to get it half open before she emerged from the shelter of the car. 'Once I'm out, I shall run for it,' she said, grinning at Tal, 'and if you get your bald patch wet, that's your problem!'

She swung her legs out of the car, opened the umbrella and ran for it. Tal closed the door, then slid out of the driving seat, slammed the door and ran after her. Large drops of rain splattered him, falling from overladen trees whose heavy branches swung in the roaring wind, and as he came out from under their comparative shelter to cross the twenty yards to the main door, the driving rain soaked the shoulders of his raincoat.

'Typical valley weather,' he grumbled to Evan, as his host met him at the door and helped him get rid of his coat.

Evan Ritchie laughed. 'Lyn's gone upstairs; she'll be down in a moment. You go in and grab yourself a whisky and soda. You'll know everyone there, I've no doubt.'

The room was large, warm, noisy and

231

crowded. The haze was part smoke and, Tal thought fancifully, part steam raised by wet collars and scorching reputations. Gatherings like these in the valley had a predilection towards the kind of gossip that was frivolous on the surface but knife-edged beneath. He tended to avoid them. This time he and Lyn had been caught.

He put on his most insincere friendly smile and advanced into the room. He made smart conversation briefly with two spinsters who served on the hospital group, then favoured a widow from the Cwmdare Trust. He undertook a sharp circumlocution with a solicitor who was already hazy in the tongue, and then he caught sight of Lyn, pinned against the wall by the greengrocer's son from Tynewydd. She had the frozen, despairing look of the recipient of a home-movie show – the greengrocer's son tended to deal in his family history conversationally. Tal rescued her; she was grateful.

'Some shindig,' she murmured, and sipped her gin and tonic. 'But everyone who *is* anyone is here.'

'We're moving in high society,' Tal agreed.

'Everything all right?' Evan Ritchie asked, moving up to them and smiling benignly. 'Enough to drink? Sandwiches in the corner, you know.'

'Great,' Tal acknowledged. 'Everyone here, then?'

'Just one or two to come,' Evan said breezily. 'But you're almost the last. All the Hospital people, and most of the Cwmdare Trust group. I was talking to one of them, by the way – she reckoned someone ought to keep an eye on the cottages. Kids have got in, or something. Smoke coming from a chimney yesterday.'

'The cottages still belong to the Trust, don't they?' Lyn asked.

'Think so. Elias is going to pay, but I'm not clear when, exactly. Anyway, must circulate...'

He circulated. Tal watched him drift from group to group, dispensing charm, liquor and sandwiches in equal amounts. He'd make it in Abercrwys. The bedside manner he'd developed as a doctor could serve well enough for a politician. Tal watched his smooth features as he put on his plastic smile. He was no longer wearing the plaster on his jawline, but there was no sign of the scratch it had hidden previously. Tal guessed he had covered it with some form of make-up – whenever Ritchie cut himself shaving he took steps to cover up the scars. Proud of his appearance, he was. Proud of his photograph in the *Echo,* too, no doubt.

'Elias,' Lyn said in a subdued tone.

'Eh?'

Lyn nudged him to be careful, and Tal sipped his whisky, turned his head slowly to glance with a studied casualness around the room. He was unable to avoid Elias's eyes. Elias was staring right at Tal: his eyes were flinty and his broad, rather brutal mouth was twisted in a sensuous, confident grin. He had the kind of heavy, powerful face that many women found attractive; his chin was pitted, his skin bad, and yet there was something about the man – an urgency, a drive – that was impressive. As Tal stood summing him up he had the impression that Tommy Elias was doing the same to him, however, and there was nothing friendly in the weighing-up process.

His blonde wife was standing near him – the same regulation two feet, Tal noticed. Close enough to establish ownership, not close enough to be uncomfortable. She was well away, too; either she had seized the opportunity to knock back a fair amount of Evan's free drink already, or else she had laid a foundation before she came. Lyn must have guessed what he was thinking.

'I understand,' she whispered, 'she has a drink problem. Can't get enough!'

An hour later Tal consulted his watch, wondering what time it would be decent to slip away. Lyn was involved at the moment with the estate agent with the ingrowing toenails and, Tal suspected, being called upon to venture a professional opinion on his incipient varicose veins. It was an occupational hazard for the medical profession – parties degenerated into consultations, free of charge. He'd try to break that up as soon as he could, and then they'd both make their apologies to Evan.

Next moment Tal forgot about Lyn, as Ieuan James entered the room.

Evan had not mentioned he was invited but he was obviously expecting him, for he came forward to greet him, shaking his hand and smiling in a self-satisfied way as James obviously offered him a congratulatory message. Evan grabbed a drink for him as they stood talking together animatedly, but James was an old hand at socializing; he talked with Evan, but his glance flitted around the room, taking in faces, noting acquaintances, checking names. Then he saw Tal.

There was no apparent change in his

expression, but his glance rested on Tal and stayed there for a split second longer than it had on others. Tal was satisfied: Ieuan James had something to report.

Involuntarily, Tal looked back towards Tommy Elias. The businessman was no longer watching Tal; instead, his eyes were fixed on the newest arrival. It was impossible to say whether the quality of the glance had changed, but Elias had certainly noted James's arrival and was interested in seeing him here.

Tal replenished his drink. The arrangement was that he should drive himself and Lyn, she would take just one gin and settle for soft drinks thereafter, and she would drive back, picking up her car at his house. So another whisky was in order. He manoeuvred himself into a quiet corner and managed to avoid circulating drinkers. Within five minutes Ieuan James had managed, apparently casually, to position himself in Tal's corner.

'Dr Rees.' He put out a hand; Tal shook it. 'Nice to see you again.' His voice dropped conspiratorially. 'I can't stay long, I'm afraid, but I thought it would be useful if I could have a quick chat with you. About the business you came to me with.'

'Ah.' Tal leaned back against the wall. He

glanced around. There was no one in earshot if they kept their voices low. Quietly he asked, 'Have your contacts managed to find out anything?'

'Depends how you look at it,' James said. His smile was enigmatic. 'They've put some work in, that's for sure.'

'To what effect?'

'Well, that's it.' James looked about him, nodded, smiled, then turned back to Tal. 'First of all, this girl. It's certainly true that she was employed by Elias at his offices in Cardiff but that's all there would seem to be to it. All the digging that's been done, discreetly, has come up with precisely nothing. As far as we've been able to discover, there is nothing to suggest Elias and Barbara Porelli had enjoyed any sort of … relationship.'

'They were both from the valley.'

'Coincidence, it would seem. In fact, she was sacked by Elias about a week before she was killed – perhaps a little more. He wasn't satisfied with the way she worked, I understand. It may be she went off somewhat annoyed, but there's no report of any kind of scene, or anything like that.'

'Was he in the area the night she died?'

James's eyes widened a trifle. He shook his head. 'I've no information on that. The … ah

'… researchers weren't able to find out what he was doing the night the girl was killed.'

With unwonted testiness, Tal clucked his tongue. 'You don't seem to have got very much from your *researchers*, Mr James.'

Ieuan James sipped his drink thoughtfully. 'That depends on how you look at things, Dr Rees. You suggest that to find nothing is *negative*. There is a positive aspect to it as well, though. Take the financial angle, for instance. What was it your informant told you about Elias's financial position?'

'Much the same as yours, isn't it, Mr James?'

Both men were startled by the interruption. Neither had noticed Lyn coming across the room to join them, but Tal was also surprised by the shine in her eyes. It was a compound of an uncharacteristic malice and a release of tension. She had not been drinking, for their arrangement about driving back stood, but she was certainly fired by Ieuan James's presence. He stared at her coolly now, a long way removed from the charmer he had been in her company on the last occasion.

'Good evening, Dr Morgan. I didn't quite catch your drift.'

'Odd,' she said, smiling wickedly. 'If *Economic News* can carry an article about you this week, I would have thought you'd know exactly what I was alluding to.'

'Well, *I* don't,' Tal said.

'I'll have to admit I picked it up in the hairdresser's,' Lyn said. 'I mean, it's not my usual reading matter – and why the hell it should appear in the *hairdresser's?* Still … but why don't *you* tell Dr Rees, Mr James? You know more about it than I do, after all.'

'I imagine you're referring to the Clwyd contract,' James said stiffly.

'That's it! Well, explain away, I'm not really very interested in financial matters,' Lyn said, and walked back across the crowded room.

Tal felt it necessary to apologize for her conduct. James watched her walk away, but appeared neither angry nor mollified. It was as though he was impervious to such remarks, and yet he *had* reacted, Tal knew.

'It's all right,' James said. 'I've read the article. The fact is, I've had a running battle for some months with Clwyd – the design of eight of my 1962 projects has come under attack for the use of high alumina cement in the structures. My argument is I built to specifications acceptable in the industry at the time. Clwyd are suing, anyway. That's the gist of the article. I'm not worried about the whole thing. It'll be cleared.'

'I ought to explain,' Tal said. 'I think Lyn is angry about the information you supplied to Evan Ritchie, and the effect it's had – Mal Powers's resignation, I mean. She's getting at me as much as at you.'

'Because you asked me to dig into Elias's background? How much does she know about your theories, then?'

'Not a great deal. And I should add I didn't like the way Ritchie handled the planning matter over the hospital, either.'

James nodded. 'I'm sorry about Powers. But I did tell Evan that they were rumours only – and difficult to prove in a court of law.'

'The valley is its own court.'

'Yes, well, anyway, to return to Elias. Your information is–?'

'That he had a cash flow problem in the wake of the building industry collapse,' Tal said. 'That he was on the verge of bankruptcy. That he was in deep financial trouble which was cumulative – the next months could see the breakdown on his industrial briquettes system unless he obtained new adequate funding, which the banks wouldn't give him.'

'I see.' Ieuan James glanced around the room again contemplatively. 'That's what I mean about the positive side, you see.'

'How do you mean?'

James looked directly at Tal. 'What you've just told me simply isn't true.'

'My informant–'

'Was wrong. To put it charitably.'

'But–'

'Look at the facts, Dr Rees. The Cwmdare Trust has recently been putting pressure on Elias over the cottages below the tip. He's just shelled out over eighteen thousand pounds, *cash,* to buy them off. Is that the action of a man with a cash flow problem? I think not. And my investigators tell me your information is far from correct. Elias, financially, has few worries. And he's far from going to the wall.'

'I don't understand...' Tal muttered.

James shrugged. 'Simple enough, really. Your informant – whoever he was – was mistaken. Or ... *he was lying.*'

Tal stared at Ieuan James and frowned. What reason would Colin Owen have for lying to him? He had admitted to being Barbara's lover, and father of the child she carried – why should he lie about the firm in which Barbara had worked?

'Anyway,' James said quietly, 'there it is. I've discovered no connection between Elias and the girl, and there's no financial problem either. So maybe you'll have to settle for Willy Thatch after all.'

'Dai Ponies,' Tal muttered.

'Pardon?'

'I know someone who can tell me the truth.'

James drained his glass. 'Ah, well, that may be. I've got my sources, no doubt you've got yours. It's up to you to tap them ... I must be on my way, Dr Rees.'

'What about the fees for your *researchers?*'

James grinned affably. 'On the house. Maybe it'll make up in some way for the Mal Powers thing. I'll be seeing you, Dr Rees...'

James moved back towards the group near the doorway comprising Evan Ritchie and the Cwmdare Trust. He was about to make his goodbyes. Lyn was in the far corner, her back somehow expressing disapproval that Tal should be talking to James at all. Beyond her was Tommy Elias.

He was still staring at Tal, and now there was open hostility in his glance.

Tal turned to the window. The curtains were drawn back and the night was black outside, but rain glistened on the window-panes as the wind drove it slanting against the house. Why did Colin Owen lie? Tal was puzzled. Either Colin Owen had lied, or else

Ieuan James was wrongly informed. Elias was aware of *something* going on – Tal could feel it in his bones. There was the possibility that James's 'researchers' had been indiscreet, and Elias had got to know of their interest in his affairs. He *could* have covered up his financial tracks; and if James was wrong about that, maybe he was wrong, also, about Elias's personal involvement with Barbara Porelli.

Dai Ponies had been so definite about it, after all. An older man. Jack Arthur had thought, maybe, a married man. Lyn had suggested such a man might be anxious about his career rather than his marriage. And Barbara had said the man she wanted to see had money. But who was it? And whoever it was, had he been at the Patch when Barbara died?

The answer lay with Dai Ponies. Wherever *he* was. Not at the pit, that was for sure. With his bronchitis, he had sought somewhere warmer and drier on the mountain. A barn, Lyn had thought, or…

Abruptly, Tal turned, finished his drink, set down his glass. Ieuan James had gone, Elias was laughing with the man on his right, Lyn was turning away and heading towards Tal, a certain sheepishness in her manner. Tal raised his hand.

She came across. 'Tal, I'm sorry, I don't know what got into me. It was just that seeing you getting involved with that man James–'

'Can you make your own way home?' Tal asked.

She opened her mouth in surprise, but Tal turned and caught Evan Ritchie's eye. 'Evan–' Ritchie came across, disengaging himself from the group he was with. 'Evan, can you drive Lyn home at the end of the evening?'

'Of course,' Evan said in surprise. 'But–'

'I've got to go.'

'What ever for?' Lyn asked. 'I'll come with you.'

'No. I'm not going home. I'm going up to Cwmdare.'

'*Cwmdare?*' Lyn said in astonishment. 'What the hell are you going up there for?'

'And on a night like this?' Evan added.

'You said earlier that someone had seen smoke coming from the chimney of one of the cottages,' Tal said quickly. 'Well, I don't think it was children who had broken in. I think it's Dai Ponies. He's got bronchitis – I told him to find somewhere warmer and drier. Now the Trust have given up the cottages, sold them to Elias, Dai's moved in.'

'You're surely not going up there to check on his bronchitis on a night like this?' Evan exclaimed. 'Tal, for God's sake, have another drink. Philanthropy is all right but—'

'It's not that,' Lyn said sharply. 'He has a theory.'

'I've got to go,' Tal said.

'A theory,' Lyn said, and the sharpness was turning to a cold annoyance. 'He thinks Barbara Porelli was attacked but not killed by Willy Thatch. He thinks there was a mysterious lover on the Patch that night. And he thinks Dai Ponies will supply the name of that lover.'

Tal turned to go. Evan put a restraining hand on his arm. 'Really, Tal? This is preposterous! You're not going all the way up there on such a crazy errand? You must be in your cups – so drink deeper, for God's sake, and forget such nonsense.'

'No, I've got to go—'

'Tal, this is obsessional!'

'And you're at a party, Tal.' Evan's voice had dropped. Tal looked at him and the anxiety in Evan's eyes flickered, disappeared. But his jaw was stiff, the line of the scratch mark appearing faintly beneath the concealing ointment he had used to salve his pride of appearance. 'Ieuan James has gone. If you go, people will start to think the party's breaking up.'

'Don't bother to see me out,' Tal said brusquely, not prepared to argue his decision. He waited for a moment, and Evan's hand dropped reluctantly away. But the half-veiled, anxious hostility in his eyes remained.

Tal left the room, walking into the cloakroom and collected his raincoat. The small window of the cloakroom shook noisily as the wind rose, hammered against the glass and dashed a gust of rain against the pane. Tal put on his coat, turned up his collar and walked out of the cloakroom.

Tommy Elias stood outside, as though barring his way.

The wide mouth was stiff and the eyes hard. Elias was a stocky, powerfully-built man, and he stood now, half crouching, like an ape about to swing into action. He was staring straight at Tal as though calculating, weighing him up, and his glance took in Tal's raincoat and manner.

'Is that the bog in there?' he asked, gesturing towards the cloakroom.

Tal shook his head. 'Upstairs.'

Elias made no move to step aside. 'Leaving early, is it?'

'That's right.'

'Pretty wet out. Be better to stay here in the warm. Got a patient, have you, Dr Rees?'

'Something like that.'

Tal stepped forward, and with a certain reluctant hesitation Elias moved aside. It was as though he wanted to say something to Tal, and it was rooted in anger, but he was not certain whether it would be wise to speak. Instead, he stood at the foot of the stairs, making no attempt to ascend them, and watched Tal walk to the door.

When Tal turned to close the door behind him the wind and rain was at his back; through the opening he saw Tommy Elias still standing watching him, and in the doorway to the lounge was the anxious figure of Evan Ritchie.

The windscreen wipers beat out a steady rhythm as the rain slanted in the headlights of the car like slivers of shining glass, shattered under the impact of the wind. Tal fancied he could hear the drumming of water on the roof even above the roar of the engine, as he negotiated the hill which swung in a long curving sweep towards the mountain road leading up to the junction where he would turn right for Cwmdare.

It was as though he was alone in a wind-swept, rainswept world, encased in the steamy car, but subjected to the battering of the gale outside until the vehicle rocked and lurched on the open road. There had been a couple of cars down at the valley floor, people swishing their way homewards with headlights blazing, but once he had turned off to cross the Pont Newydd bridge it was as though he had left all civilization behind him and there was only the mountain and the darkness and the wind.

He could see very little. The road ribboned away from him, the white line gleaming under the headlights, and he received vague impressions of trees and crags and bridges overhanging the road, but though he knew the route well the darkness shrouded it with unfamiliarity so that he almost felt he was travelling in an unknown world, where distances were impossible to calculate, where bends and hills were totally unexpected, where gradients seized his car engine before he had time to change gear. It was something he had not experienced before in the valley, and as he peered through the rainswept windscreen it was with the feeling that the valley itself had changed: it was no longer the warm secure place that had succoured him in his emotional agonies but a hostile place full of malignancy and foreboding.

The feeling became more positive when he crossed the hill and turned into Cwmdare.

In a way he had never accepted the reputation the cwm had enjoyed for fifty years. To Tal, it had simply been a pleasant enough little valley, where stories of the old disasters gave rise to fanciful tales on the part of old men eager to impress youngsters with prickling accounts of death and destruction in the darkness of a rat-ridden, dripping shaft. But under the darkness of night it had lost its familiarity, and he was more ready to believe in its malignancy, more ready to accept the anthropomorphic concepts that valley folk held of its destructive qualities and intentions towards the people who dared to enter the confines of the shrouding hills. It was as though it lay there like some half-seen, monstrous nightmare beast, with its arms held wide to embrace the traveller who entered its realm, and the wind and rain that tore and howled across the steep slopes of the hill was the symphonic background against which it acted out its evil destiny.

It had taken men's lives in the distant past and now it was alive again, roaring, its maw open as Tal drove the shuddering car along the winding track that led into the heart of the cwm.

Down to his left was the old tram track where the coal had been run down to the valley floor; ahead of him in the darkness under the hill was the Dare Pit with its broken-backed wheelhouse and half-buried, rusted boilers, and at the head of the narrow road that he now followed was the slope which swung up towards the cottages the Cwmdare Trust had purchased and Tommy Elias had now bought from the trustees.

Elias.

Tal could still see the hostility in his glance as he had stood staring across the crowded room. Ieuan James's snoopers must have been indiscreet, and Elias would have known that Tal was asking questions about him. But was he the man whom Barbara Porelli had gone to meet at the Patch?

Dai Ponies could help answer that question. If Tommy Elias had tumbled the schoolgirl in the ferns those years ago, there was the possibility that it was he whom she had wanted to blackmail. It was an ugly word, but it fitted. She had wanted money, not marriage; independence, not a forced marital tie with the son of Cyfarthfa Owen.

But why had Colin lied? If James was right, and Owen *had* lied, there was the possibility that he had lied about other matters too – such as Barbara refusing to meet him. Owen admitted to having been in the valley on the night she died; perhaps he had been at the Patch...

The car slid to a stop. Tal engaged the brake, pushed the gear lever into first gear, tried to pull away. He felt rather than heard the wheels spin, and the car shuddered, but it stayed where it was on the slope. Tal put the lever into neutral, huddled deeper into his raincoat and opened the car door. He stepped out and the wind grabbed at him, thrust him against the side of the car with a great wet fist, and slammed the breath out of his chest. He stood there for a moment with his back to the car, head down, trying to recover his breath, and then in the headlights he saw the mass of slime that lay thickly across the road, black and semi-liquid. He looked up and saw where the bank had given way, the oak tree that had fallen athwart the hedge, and the dirt still washing down across the road. The slurry lay everywhere, perhaps twenty feet in area, and the car wheels took no purchase in the stuff.

If Taliesin Rees expected to visit Dai Ponies this night, he would have to walk to do it.

Tal left the side lights on the car on, so

that the vehicle should not prove a hazard to anyone else driving up – not that there would be anyone. But leaving the lights on would also help him find his way back to the car in the rain and the darkness. With his left hand clutching at his collar, protecting his throat, and his head bowed, Tal walked through the slurry and over the rim of the slope, half-bent, like the old farmer from Treharris whose arthritic joints had made a six-foot figure into one of four feet eight.

The wind and rain buffeted at Tal as he came over the slope and he could hear the rushing of water to his left where what had earlier been a small brook now raged as a six-feet wide torrent. Thirty yards on, and still climbing steadily, the wind suddenly dropped and Tal could raise his head under the rain: he was in the lee of the hill and the wind no longer dashed at him. More happily, he could see the dim outline of a wall – the wall which would lead him up to the cottages. Tal took a deep breath and hurried on.

He was cold, and water no longer trickled down his neck – instead, he felt a numbness along his back which suggested that his raincoat was no longer keeping out the driving rain. He hurried on, felt the gravel of the track that Tommy Elias had laid for his lorries crunch under his feet, and some thirty yards further on he stumbled against the open gate of the first of the cottages. It was wide, swinging and banging crazily in the wind, but Tal could hardly see the outline of the cottage itself. His eyes were blurred with the rain and he put out his hand like a blind man, feeling his way over the grass-ridden flagstones that led up to the cottage door.

He stumbled against the door and it opened under his hand.

The wind and the rain raged against the old stone of the cottage, but inside it was like the eye of the hurricane, strangely quiet, dark, almost menacing in its stillness, with only the small creaking sounds of age and decay to betray the fact of its existence. There was a faint odour of faded musk, dry death, a whisper of corruption; the rustling sounds that came from deep in the darkness were like the soft calling of people long gone, disturbed now by the violence of the night at Tal's back. There was dust here, a carpet of dirt, broken furniture, but the only life existed among the mice and the beetles and the spiders, soundless in the darkness.

Outside, the wind hurtled spears of icy rain at the walls.

It was the same feeling in the second cottage and the third. Tal entered each one, feeling the dark emptiness of the cottage greet him with what seemed like a close, dusty warmth in contrast to the battering wind outside. But though he called, raising his voice against the wail of the elements outside, there was nothing but a faded echo, a reverberation of his own voice, a disturbance of an atmosphere, a scurrying in dark corners.

But when he entered the fourth cottage he sensed immediately that it was different. To begin with, he had some difficulty opening the door. It was as though something had been wedged against it in an attempt to encourage its resistance to the gale. None of the cottages had been locked; the Trust had not found it necessary to place padlocks on the cottage doors when they had bought them because there was little risk of vandalism – the cwm was not a popular place with children, and the young thugs preferred tearing up the local dance halls to breaking down already dilapidated cottages on the hillside. But Tal had to put his shoulder against the door and heave to force it open. It finally gave way with a light, cracking, splintering sound that told him he had forced away the doorpost from the wall; he struggled in, forcing his shoulders through the gap, and when his eyes cleared from the wetness of the rain and grew accustomed to the dimness inside the cottage, he was able to make out vaguely a bundle, a pile of rubbish, old clothing by the feel of it, timber, rubbish, piled against the door in an attempt to keep it closed and retain the warmth of the cottage.

'Dai?'

His voice sounded restricted and un-natural, a hoarse croak that skittered upwards like a frightened crow under the eaves of the house, darting into the dark corners of the room, fading in the darkness.

'Dai Ponies!' Even before the echo had crashed away into silence, Tal tried again. 'Are you there, Dai? Are you there?' The words tumbled over each other eagerly, scrambling for the anonymous safety of the rickety stairs that led up to the one bedroom above. But there was no sound when they had gone, only the howling wind beyond the door, the rain spattering against boarded-up windows, the rattling of the roof under the violence of the storm.

Yet he was here; Tal *knew* he was here. It was a tangible knowledge, he could almost *feel* Dai's presence here in the cottage, in the way he had sometimes felt the presence of

Death in a hospital ward, or in a quiet terrace house where an old miner slipped away with glazing, thankful eyes. And that was it, Tal suddenly realized: this was a hospital ward, a darkened death room, the slightly sweet atmosphere, cloying to the nostrils, that denoted a place of death. His hand was shaking slightly as he stumbled forward, began to move around the black room with outstretched hands, seeking for the thing he was reluctant to find.

He reached the wall, touched it, leaned against it. He began to move around, skirting the wall. He reached the stairwell, moved past it, felt the old black-leaded grate that had served for hot water supply, cooker, and fireplace in those older, less expansive times, and he put his hand into the grate. There was rubbish in there, charred timber, and he felt the smoky softness marking his fingers, but it was probably imagination only that made him think the grate was still warm.

Then his foot struck something that yielded, tumbled sideways with a noise as light as the scamper of mice in the darkness. Tai stood still for a long moment and his heartbeat was quick with the unreasoning fear that an old house and a dark violent night could bring. He put out his foot again, felt the softness of thick blanketing clothes and slowly he went down on his knees. He put out his right hand; the exploring fingers felt an old ragged coat, a torn blanket, a pile of oddments that would have given warmth. But not enough warmth. The face above them was cold.

Tal squatted on his heels as he had seen all those miners squat in the days of the Depression. The sunlight seemed to have shone on them, and the faces of those young men had been tanned in a way they rarely were during summer months. But the tans had not masked the hopelessness in those faces, and Dai Ponies had been one of those men. But those days were long gone for him now; there were no more days. Tal searched slowly in his pockets for the box of matches he carried, a habit he had not lost in spite of twenty years without smoking. The matches rattled as he drew out the box; the first matchstick broke, the second spluttered, flared, and Tal lifted the match away from his eyes, allowing the faint light to fall on the bundle that lay in front of him.

Dai Ponies had been dead for some hours.

He seemed even smaller now than he had when alive. The rags were piled around him, up to his chin, and yet his body seemed to be outlined under the clothing, lacking in the hard muscularity that Tal remembered, now just small and vulnerable. His eyes were wide open, but there seemed to be no flesh on his face, and his lips, which had always been thin and bloodless, were now thin stretched lines along an open mouth, crying soundlessly for the help that had not come.

Tal rocked lightly on his heels. An immense, painful depression gripped him; it was as though his own life was crumbling away just as Dai Ponies's life had gone. Failure and desolation lay all around him: Barbara Porelli, Willy Thatch, Dai Ponies – and even Lyn too – he had failed them all in some way or another. To each of them he could have held out a helping hand; Barbara might not have died if he had probed more, tried to help her more positively; Willy Thatch would not have confessed and then hanged himself if only Tal had kept the promise to Willy's wife and gone to see him; Lyn wanted only a word from him and he had been unable to give it to her – and Dai Ponies had been up here for days, in the darkness of the cottage, dying from bronchitis in the lonely, insistently independent manner that Tal should have broken down.

But now it was too late. The old man was

dead, and all the stories he could tell about the mountainside and the ferns, the pitheads and the valley, they were gone with him. He could have told Tal who Barbara Porelli's lover had been those years ago, but not now – and somehow it seemed not to matter. Tal had come up here for a selfish reason, to satisfy the demands of his own ego, but in coming he had discovered yet another failing to bruise his own soul. He should have come up to Cwmdare to help Dai Ponies, not to question him, and now it was too late.

He saw Taliesin Rees clearly now, for what he was, and he did not like what he saw.

But that was the whole problem, really. One never did see the truth until it was too late. There were images, projections upon a hazy screen, vague, confused, diffused pictures where a man saw himself and the others only as actors in a drama, where the truth lay concealed beneath layers and veneers, strata of self-deception.

Yet he of all people should never have been confounded by such images. It was many years now since he had spoken to that old woman in Caergwent, as she lay dying in the hospital. She had told him then, in words that haunted his conscious life for many years and dictated his compassion, his course of conduct, his practice of medicine in the valley. She had torn away some of the veils of self-deception he had donned then, but over the years he had forgotten what she taught him.

Yet he could recall those words now, as though they had been spoken only yesterday.

She had peered up at him from her bed with eyes that still held the glint of the anger and determination she had been born with eighty years earlier.

'Come to witness my death, have you, Dr Rees? Young man like you, what do you know, eh? When you look at me, what do you see? Just a wrinkled, crabbed old woman, isn't it; no feelings, no emotions, everything grey and dead, nothing, nothing... But that's it, you see; it's not me you see at all, not the *real* me. Inside, it's still like I'm twenty, boy, with all the hunger for life that a young girl's got. Not men, no, perhaps I don't have that knife in me that calls for a man, but the rest of it, the loving part and the wanting part, that hasn't changed. So don't come here looking at me as you *think* I am; try to remember that it is a shell you are looking at, *bach*, and the person inside hasn't changed for sixty years. Don't look and see just the *image;* look inside, and see that it's different, because that's what the truth is, *inside*, not the image lying here. Be sure you know what it is you are witnessing, Dr Rees. Not an old woman, dying, but a life that was young and never really changed, not *inside*...'

He had witnessed many deaths since, and had remembered. It was what had made him different as a doctor, and brought him respect. He had never had patients, only friends, for he had *cared*. But in caring, at last he had forgotten too. The roots of his caring had gone, they had become an indulgence, and he no longer *saw* the people inside. The old woman of Caergwent had shown him the road but for a while he had forgotten it.

So he must look again at Dai Ponies. And at Lyn.

And at all the other images.

But even as the thought crossed his mind it was superseded by another, flashing realization that it was too late. For there was a wild, high, cracking sound and the darkness seemed to leap at him, slamming him backwards against the cottage wall and the pain seared across his chest and side like the icy knife of death.

The house was alive after all the dead years. They were gathered in the dark corners, whispering, generations of miners and their families who had lived and died in Cwmdare. They clustered together and watched and whispered, their voices old and rusty, creaking like twigs underfoot on a frosty morning, calling to Tal, telling him the way, but in words he could hear yet not understand. They sought the protection of the house from the malignancy of the cwm as it reached out for them in the rain and the storm. For it was almost done, the cwm had taken almost its final revenge, and soon, in a matter of hours, the last trace of men could be washed away from the hillside.

Tal could feel the black slime under his hands. He was lying on his side, with his face upturned to the roof, but the heavy beam lay across him, pinning him to the floor, and the slurry was creeping, slithering like a live thing, a slow snake across the cottage floor. Tal knew it was mere chance he was still alive; had he been standing, the beam would have crushed his skull. Instead, it had struck him a glancing blow, fracturing several ribs, and pinning him to the ground. But Tal knew too that it was only a matter of time before Death reached out for him. The slurry had finally given way under the heavy rain above the cottage; it had piled up against the cottage walls, caved in the roof, and now it was flowing slowly, its initial impetus lost, but infiltrating the cottage in a black tide that would soon rise, creep up past his arms and shoulders, enter his mouth and nose and eyes as he lay helpless under the beam.

He would die here with Dai Ponies, buried under the black slime the old man had predicted would come down into the cottages if the work did not stop and the rains came.

Strangely enough, Tal felt at peace with himself for the first time in weeks … perhaps months. It was probably because he was helpless, probably because he knew there was nothing he could do to help or save himself. But inside him there was also a small satisfaction – he would die soon, but at least he had seen the truth again, heard the old woman of Caergwent, torn aside the veiling images and sought for what lay beyond. He knew now he had deluded himself for years; the old agonies of the loss of his wife had been buried as he was about to be buried; he had come to depend upon Lyn in the way she had depended on him, and though he would never tell her so, not now, at least he knew the way he felt about her. And Willy Thatch, and Barbara Porelli, and the rest of it, symptoms only of the disease that had struck him, a disease compounded of self-doubt and self-torture. The answer had never really lain with Dai Ponies, it had lain within men's minds. People saw only what they were taught to see and expected to see – the images were the thing.

And the images were stripped away for Tal now, for he was close to death, and life was a region of clarity that he'd soon be leaving. The images – the *real* images – were sharp.

The creaking voices faded under the sharp cracking sound as another beam gave way, there was a roaring sound in Tal's ears and then a gush of black slurry surged into the room. It settled, slurping around his lower body, and silence crept back. His head sagged and he listened for the voices but they did not return; he listened for the wind and the rain but they seemed no longer to carry, and for one brief second he thought he was dead.

But then he knew the rain had stopped, and the wind had softened in the cwm and there was only the silence of the darkness outside, and the slow seeping gurgle of the slurry drifting down the hill.

It was an unreal time. There was a sharp stabbing pain in his chest as he struggled to breathe, lifting his chest against the dead weight of the heavy beam, and perhaps he slept, for when he opened his eyes he thought he was imagining things. But it was not so: he could see a whitish area, circular, diffused at the edges, flickering against the far wall. Light. It danced, hesitated, dashed in an excited movement around the cottage, leaped up to the ruined stairwell, hesitated, lingered over the menacing roof as it hovered, eager to collapse under the growing weight and pressure of the slurry pushing against the cottage walls.

Then it dropped to Tal's face, pinned him in its brightness, dazzled his staring eyes.

'I'm here,' Tal gasped, 'I'm alive!'

The unwinking eye of the torch examined him dispassionately, unmoved. It held his anguished face for several seconds before it moved away, flickering around the cottage again, probing, searching for something. Tal opened his mouth to call for help again, but then closed it, for he *knew*. The voice came as though from a great distance and perhaps it was, in terms of involvement and compassion.

'Did you find him?'

Tal made no reply for a moment. The beam of the torch slipped back to him demandingly, and too weak to deny its strength Tal closed his eyes, nodded wearily.

'Yes.'

'In this cottage?'

The torchlight flashed about again, seeking. It lingered beside the fireplace, half buried in the slime. It picked out the bundle of clothing that lay there, half covered.

'Is that him?'

The pain stabbed at Tal's chest.

'Yes,' he gasped. 'He's dead. You've nothing to fear from Dai Ponies. He died up here alone in the darkness. You've no longer need to fear him.'

'If I ever did,' the voice came softly. 'I couldn't be sure... Perhaps he did see me with the girl years ago when I came to Lloyd Street, but it was a long time ago and over so quickly, it could have meant nothing to him, and he could point no fingers at me.'

'But you had to be sure,' Tal said. 'Just in case.'

'That's right. Just in case.'

'If he had remembered something important, what would you have done?' Tal asked.

'Whatever had to be done. But it's no longer necessary. He's dead.'

'I'm not.'

'You soon will be. When the slurry comes

266

in and smothers you.'

'You could get me out.'

'No.' The voice faded away reflectively, and the dead whispers in the corner of the room were silent as the word lingered under the broken timbers of the roof. 'No, I couldn't do that. I don't think you know very much, it was mainly guesswork on your part, but I couldn't be sure that you wouldn't make more of it all after speaking to that old man dead there in the corner. So when you left the party it was necessary that I followed you. There's too much at stake, far too much at stake for you to spoil things now. I couldn't take the chance. But when I go back down to the valley there'll be no chance left. You, Dai Ponies, the girl … all gone. Everything clear. At last.'

'You *did* kill her, then.'

The torchlight wavered slightly and there was a short silence. Then there was a sigh. 'Not in the way I was prepared to kill you. Funny, that. I suppose it's because it's easier the second time. When I arranged to meet her at the Patch I was going to threaten her, make her see sense, maybe bruise her a bit. As a last resort, I was prepared to try to buy her silence. She had this silly idea – she was in love with that Owen boy, you know, but wanted to save him by *not* marrying him. Funny, isn't it? Prepared to blackmail me to gain herself freedom from the need to marry a man she loved but might have destroyed in the long run. Twisted motives, that girl.'

'She was an independent.'

'Aye... But she was a real problem for me. But killing ... I hadn't thought of that. Not until she came into the Patch and I was waiting against the wall and that great oaf came up behind her, grabbed her, and she fought him. He knocked her down, stood over her as though puzzled, not knowing what to do...'

Tal could see the picture in the darkness of the Patch. Willy Thatch, big, shambling, drunk, vaguely aware of the enormity of his attack upon the girl, lust retreating, puzzled...

'He even started to walk away, then kicked her handbag, bent over and stole her money and shambled off. I came out of the shadows after he'd gone. I stood over her. She was just regaining consciousness. There was just a few seconds when I didn't know what to do. Then there was the solution. Clear. I thought no more about it. A knee on her chest, my fingers on her throat...'

'So ... so Willy didn't tear at her clothing, and didn't assault her sexually,' Tal said, as the pain seared in his chest.

'It was his intention to do so, but fighting her seemed to drive lust away. Then it was obvious what I had to do. The motive for murder *had* to be sex. The police would then look no further. So I tore at her underclothes, manhandled her body. And the police fell for it. Motive: sexual gratification. And Willy Thatch, the great, drunken fool, he set the seal on it...'

A confession dragged from hazy memories, fed by police suggestion. He had been the perfect subject for the occasion.

'And it could have stayed all right, it could have ended there, but for you... *Everything* else was working out. Mal Powers's position was weakened and his support dwindling; the hospital project was going to get its approval, with all that meant for me; Willy Thatch was blamed for the death of the girl and there was no way, no reason, in which any connection could be made with me. It was neat, pieces fitting into place, the furniture looking clear at last. But you wouldn't let things lie. The infuriating thing was you were going off in the wrong direction, reaching wrong conclusions, thinking it was simply a matter of sex behind Barbara Porelli's death. But you were still asking questions, probing in corners, digging... The chances are you'd have found nothing, because the questions were wrong... But it was a chance I couldn't afford to take. Not with all that money at stake.'

'Money?'

The torch became impatient, stabbed at the darkness in a sudden, uncontrolled violence. 'That bitch, she saw us together. It was essential that we were not connected, that we remained unknown to each other officially, but she was there in the office one day, and she saw me. I didn't know then ... I discovered *later* that she was working at the Cardiff office and I got her fired, just in case she ever discovered the connection. But even so, I didn't realize how dangerous she could be.'

The torch wavered hesitantly, flickered around the walls, probed at the creaking beams and sought out the creeping slurry on the floor. 'When I knew her years ago, she was just a kid, a sex-hungry kid... But she'd grown up. And she had teeth. She was quick and smart, and in the time she worked in the Cardiff office she learned enough about the financial problems of the whole industry to begin to put things together. She talked to Colin Owen and she told him, but he wasn't smart enough to put two and two together the way she did. When she rang me, insisted on seeing me, and we made the arrangement for the Patch meeting, I knew she had me over a barrel. She had looked deep into the business, unravelled some of the skein, the web of contacts in the vale. She didn't know the *details* but she knew enough to cause the right questions to be asked, questions that would put me in deep water. Contacts and kick-backs and contracts ... she guessed at the game.' The voice slowed, became reflective. 'She didn't really know anything. Like you. But she had questions. And threats. And to her it was all so simple. She had seen us together; she knew we had some sort of contact even though we'd publicly denied it. From that time when she came back to the office and saw us together, she began to put pieces into slots. Money, public denials, contracts, bankruptcy, cash flow ... she was smart enough to get the general picture. Uncomfortable. In the way your questions became uncomfortable. Questions ... I killed her because of the questions she had in her mind ... now, you...'

The torch left Tal's face in a nervous, searching flicker. It danced around the room, its brightness probing the corners, and Tal's head dropped. He was exhausted, but it was emotional as much as physical.

'I could leave you,' the voice whispered. 'That tip up there, it's full of water. The slurry is drifting down; the pressure at the back of the cottage is bound to sweep the whole structure down to the valley floor. But how long will it take? It could happen in a matter of minutes. But the rain has stopped and it could take hours to collapse the cottage. Soon, that woman Dr Morgan might look for you. Your car's down there in the road. Come morning they'll see the damage to the cottages ... and you could still be here ... alive...'

The torch light stopped, picked out the five-feet length of timber in the corner of the room, fixed on it, whitened it in its brightness.

'I can't take the chance.' The light dropped, there was a scrambling sound as the man moved forward to pick up the heavy timber, and then he turned, his back to the rear wall and the stairwell, the torch in his left hand, the timber in his right.

'I can't take the chance, Dr Rees. If your head is crushed it'll be no more than the state of your ribs. It could have happened in a fall. So they'll say you didn't have to wait for the slow, choking death from the slurry.

Your death was quick, a roof fall…'

'You're mad! You can't do this–'

'I did it once. I killed Barbara Porelli, and the decision to do so was swift, unthinking. But this time, though it's deliberate, it's not difficult, Dr Rees. The whole thing has a sort of pattern to it, a satisfying end to a series of problems that have dogged me for five years and more. When you die, Dr Rees, I can start to put the pieces together again…'

He put down the torch with a slow deliberate movement. Its unwinking eye shone on Tal's face. The man stood tall, grasping the timber in both hands. As it was lifted, it was lost to Tal's sight. He was aware of the man standing above him with the timber raised, ready to bring crashing down on his defenceless head.

And suddenly the silence was gone. From the corner came all those silenced voices, the dead whispers of yesteryear, the men and the women and the children who had been born and lived and died in this cottage and this cwm, and they raised their voices in warning and in threats, and the creaking turned to a screaming, a rushing, roaring noise that filled the ears and the senses, the sound of violence from a thousand dead throats. The torch leapt and twisted under the sound, flickered one wild glance of light into the staring eyes of Ieuan James before the old timbers of the stairwell rose under the surging of the mountain, and the raking spears pierced him and threw him, screaming soundlessly, directly at Tal's terrified head.

3

Days later, with the uniforms, and the polished floor, and the bright sunlight streaming through the high windows of the hospital ward, it was a world away from the darkness and violence and malevolence of Cwmdare. But as Tal waited for Lyn to join him to complete her round of the other ward, his mind drifted back, involuntarily to that night, and there was a cooling of his blood, a sudden shudder as he recalled the long hours of darkness before the lights came up the cwm, friendly lights, so unlike the malignant beam of Ieuan James's torch. Tal had lain there during those black hours, waiting for death, with Ieuan James's dead body half suffocating him, and the cold, deadly slurry thickly liquid about his neck and shoulders. The old house had been silent, waiting with him for the Old Reaper to come again, but he had not come.

There had been time to think, to try to avoid the panic that could choke him, drive life from his body in a wild struggle for survival that could end in disaster. There had been time to remember Colin Owen, unable to understand how Barbara could love him so much that she wanted to cut free from him; time to remember how the girl had said she would sort things out for herself; time to remember how Taliesin Rees had seen only images of reality projected on a screen, and failed to see the reality itself – in others or in himself. Colin Owen had told him the truth, but Tal had believed the lies of Ieuan James, the man who had killed once and sought to kill again.

And ironically enough it had been Ieuan James who had saved Tal's life. The slurry had burst through, shattering the cottage and sending a spear of timber through James's body, and Tal should have died too. But James's cooling corpse had lain across him, forming a barrier against the black slurry as it crept through the ruined cottage. The rain had stopped, the progress of the slurry had slowed, and Tal had waited in the darkness as down in the valley Lyn had become anxious that he had not returned.

At three in the morning she had persuaded Evan Ritchie to join her in a drive to Cwmdare; they had found Tal's abandoned car and James's Jaguar nearby. They had seen the ruination of the cottages and they had called the police and an ambulance, and before dawn they had all come to Cwmdare.

Lights and people and shouts, the roar of engines, the determined digging of workmen, groaning timbers and the thud of stones, they were the sounds Tal would never forget. Nor, after they had found Tal and the two dead men half buried in the slime, would he forget how Lyn had clung to his hand in the ambulance during the drive to the hospital. No questions, just a silent, committed clutching to his life. No words. They were not necessary.

Tal's injuries had not been serious. A broken collarbone and three broken ribs to add to his bruised emotions. And now he had been discharged, and was able to resume his own practice. Evan had told him at the surgery that Lyn was down at Church Village, and Tal had come down to see her. It was time he told her, at last, if he could find the right words.

When she came walking down the corridor towards him her face brightened and she smiled broadly. She said nothing but took his arm, gave it a squeeze, and led him in towards the far ward. There were three patients at the far end: one of them a young girl, lying seemingly exhausted.

'It's Jean Hughes,' Lyn said. 'She's just had her baby. They'll be bringing him in shortly... Tal, you look well this morning.'

'I'm fit, Lyn. And ready to start back.'

She squeezed his arm again. 'I'm glad. The practice isn't the same without you – even if you're missing only for a matter of days.'

'It won't be the same without *you*, Lyn.'

She looked at him steadily for a moment, then changed the subject. 'Evan rang me here, said you were coming down, but that you'd probably stop off to see Jack Arthur.'

'That's right. Just half an hour. He's ... contrite,' Tal said. 'I think he's trying to make up as much lost ground as he can. Inspector Jack Arthur is suddenly keen to have as many friends as he can possibly find, because there's to be an official inquiry by the Home Office regarding Willy Thatch's arrest, as well as his suicide. But, well, I'm pretty sure Jack will survive it. He's one of life's survivors, after all.'

'Not like poor Willy,' Lyn said quietly.

'No ... but I suppose his wife has the satisfaction of knowing that Willy's name is cleared in part, at least. All right, she has to live with the knowledge that he followed Barbara into the Patch, attacked her there, but at least he didn't *kill* her.'

'It seems little enough consolation.'

Tal nodded. 'As you say, little enough. But she's not the only one to come out of this mess with bruises. There's Mal Powers, for instance.'

Lyn wrinkled her nose in thought, and shook her head. 'I still don't understand that. I just can't see why Ieuan James behaved the way he did – why he told Evan Ritchie that tale about Mal Powers. I gather from Evan – who himself is pretty contrite, but happy enough to benefit from it all by running to his new job, for all that – the information James gave him about Mal Powers was largely unfounded. A little smoke, even less fire.'

'Three hundred pounds' worth of fire by way of bribes, it would seem. But enough to make Mal Powers resign under the threat of exposure.'

'But why did Ieuan James *do* it?' Lyn asked.

Tal shrugged. 'Jack Arthur gave me most of the story this morning, in his eagerness to please. They've had Elias sweating it out for a few days, and they've got a statement from him at last. It contains a hell of a lot of names – councillors and officials from the vale. Mal Powers was pretty small fry, according to Arthur, when compared to the others James has corrupted.'

'Was *that* what it is all about? Council corruption?'

Tal nodded emphatically. 'It would seem so. Ever since Ieuan James's wife divorced him he's been skating on thin ice. He went to the States and came an awful cropper financially, so he was near broke when he came back. But he kept up appearances. Indeed, even recently, when I went to see him in his Penarth office, I found he had a swish place there – though strangely enough I saw no staff. The truth was, there were hardly any. But James kept up the front of the successful architect and builder. The trouble was, like everybody else, he'd been hit by the recession.'

'He was headed for bankruptcy too?'

'More or less. You see, Lyn, when he returned to Wales he set out deliberately to build up his business in the only way he really knew to succeed – by bribery, by corrupting councillors and officers to put contracts his way. But local government reorganization meant he was dealing with new men after 1972 and they weren't as amenable to his approaches as his earlier contacts. At the time, he was hit hard by the recession. He still thought he could win through, when a series of financial body-blows hit him. You'll remember he told us he'd won that civic building contract in the Midlands?'

'Yes, I remember.'

'Well, what he *didn't* tell us was that they had made inquiries into his financial position, and in particular into his other commitments, and the Midland authority told him he could have that contract, provided he completed his other major commitments by 1977.'

'The Llandarog Hospital,' Lyn said thoughtfully.

'Exactly. It was essential that the Llandarog project made a start at once – only then could Ieuan James win the Midlands contract, which he was relying on to pull him clear out of the red. The trouble was–'

'The council had reversed their decision, and wanted to push the road through. And that,' Lyn said triumphantly, 'would mean considerable delay, and the loss of the Midlands contract.'

'That's about the size of it,' Tal agreed.

'That's why he fed Evan the Mal Powers information. He guessed that if Evan jumped on the bandwagon the rest of the planning committee would flee from the odour surrounding Powers and go back to their original decision – to build the hospital at Llandarog.'

'And it worked.'

'It did indeed, once Mal Powers resigned.'

'But none of this explains Barbara Porelli's part in it all,' Lyn said.

Tal nodded thoughtfully. 'It's odd, really. I was going up to see Dai Ponies because I thought the name of the man Barbara Porelli was with in the ferns years ago would be significant. It would have been – it was Ieuan James. But I wouldn't have *seen* the significance of it – though James couldn't take the chance. He was afraid that if Dai Ponies told me, I'd continue to ask questions, and everything would blow skyhigh. You see, Lyn, Barbara's involvement with James was short: one summer on the mountain, when she was in the fifth form and he was a married man, coming to visit his grandmother in Lloyd Street. It was all over that summer – until Barbara Porelli went to work for Tom Elias in Cardiff.'

'What was important about that?'

'Nothing at first. Until she saw a television programme called *Confrontation* – on which both Elias and James appeared, and when they publicly stated they did not know each other. You see, Barbara knew otherwise. Because she came back to Elias's office one night to pick up something she'd left behind, and she saw them together in Elias's office – *before* the *Confrontation* programme had been recorded.'

'But why did they deny knowing each other on television?' Lyn asked.

'That was precisely the question in Barbara's mind. It was a question that loomed larger when inexplicably she got a week's notice a few days after she saw the *Confrontation* programme. And there were other questions that came to be added. When she had met Colin Owen, and he got stuck on financial problems in Elias's firm, she looked up a few figures for him. She guessed that Elias was in financial trouble. Then she heard he was being pressed by the Cwmdare Trust for compensation for the cottages. *Then* she learned he was likely to pay. But where would he get eighteen thousand pounds with *his* cash flow problems?'

'Where indeed?'

'Ieuan James.'

'But why—'

'Let's go back a step. I said James suffered a series of financial body-blows. The first was the doubt surrounding the Midlands contract; the second was the hold-up of the Llandarog project. The third problem was the threatened suit over the contracts he'd completed using high alumina cement. He was in a *very* shaky financial position, and to top it all Elias now came to him with a demand. He wanted cash to pay off the Cwmdare Trust.'

'But what led him to expect James could or would pay him?'

'The reason why James did not want it to be common knowledge that he and Elias were business partners. The reason why he told Elias to sack Barbara Porelli. The reason why he killed Barbara Porelli, in the end. A very simple reason. Tom Elias was Ieuan James's front man for the corruption of councillors in the vale. They were tied closely, but secretly, and Elias now told James straight. Elias would go bust if he couldn't pay off the Trust. So James had to cough up. If he didn't, Elias warned him, everything would blow. Elias would go bankrupt, his affairs would be investigated, certain doubtful contracts could come to light, and Elias would sure as dammit involve Ieuan James. He'd guarantee it. So James paid up. He scoured his own coffers and gave Elias the money. And then he set to work, blackening Mal Powers, pushing through the chances of an early completion of the hospital at Llandarog, and hoping to secure the Midlands contract which would bring him financially clear – always hoping he could wriggle out of the high alumina claim.'

'And Barbara Porelli–'

'Threatened to foul the whole operation,' Tal interrupted. 'As far as I can make out, she loved Colin Owen, but felt to marry him would ruin his career. She was a realist; thought him infatuated; and though she was in love with him she was independent enough to deny her love. But she also smarted under the suspicion that James might have got her the sack, even though they had once been lovers. She was a smart girl, and the questions began to mount in her mind. She didn't *really* know what it was all about, but she guessed that if James didn't want it to be known that he and Elias were acquaintances he might be prepared to pay for her silence. That was what she meant when she left my surgery: she was going to screw money out of Ieuan James, maybe for the way he'd treated her in Cardiff. And James would probably have paid her off – if Willy Thatch hadn't stumbled into the Patch, reaching and grabbing for Barbara. And when she fell, stunned herself on the stone, he saw his chance. He told me at Cwmdare: after Willy had gone, he strangled her.'

Lyn was quiet for a moment. The sun seemed to have faded momentarily, and the ward was less bright. The young mother in the corner of the ward twisted uneasily on her bed.

'When Barbara died, he must have thought he was in the clear,' Lyn said.

'He almost was. Willy Thatch tied ends up for him neatly by killing himself. Elias had been suspicious, but accepted the story that Willy had murdered the girl, and Jack Arthur was satisfied Willy was the killer – he *had* to be, for Jack, if some of the heat was to be taken out of the inquiry into Willy's suicide.'

'The heat is back on again now.'

'As it was on Ieuan James,' Tal said grimly, 'when I began to insist Willy had not killed Barbara. I was running blind, going by the *feel* of things, and really getting nowhere. But I touched some sore spots for James, and he was worried. When I went to him he must have been relieved in a sense – by chance, I was giving him the opportunity to head me off, push me up a blind alley. He told me Elias was not involved with Barbara Porelli. That should have ended it – because, after all, I was thinking only along the lines of Barbara blackmailing her *lover*. She was, of course, blackmailing a man who had been her lover, but the reasons behind the killing were more complicated. I was a long way from the truth, I was concerned with a different image entirely, but James was afraid I would reach down to the right questions if I continued. And when I said Dai Ponies might identify the man who had first seduced Barbara Porelli, he got scared.'

'He waited for you in the rain,' Lyn said tonelessly, her eyes shadowed.

'That's right. And when I left to go to Cwmdare, he followed me. He didn't know where the old man was. I led him to Dai Ponies. And after all, James needn't have bothered. His secret was safe; Dai was dead.'

'But you were alive, and he had committed himself.'

'It's time *I* committed myself, Lyn,' Tal said quietly.

She looked at him with eyes that widened and there was a light deep in those eyes but she said nothing. He heard someone entering the ward and glanced sideways: Sister, with the baby for Jean Hughes in the corner. Lyn looked sideways too, released Tal's arm and walked with the nurse down to the bed where the young mother lay. Sister left the baby with Mrs Hughes, and the girl began to unwrap the child. Lyn stood watching, as Tal came to her side.

'I remember you saying once,' she said quietly, 'how most of medicine seems to be about pain and misery and death, but there's childbirth too, and that makes it all worth while.'

'The best part of medicine,' Tal said.

Witness my death, the old lady from Caergwent had said, but *look*. Look beyond the superficial image, look inside, deep into others, and into yourself. He had done it in the old days, and seen birth as the beautiful part of medical practice, life and reason. But he had forgotten to look deeply into people, and into himself.

'Lyn,' he said, 'Evan goes soon. Don't *you* go.'

'Tal–'

'Please. Stay with me, Lyn. In the valley.'

The girl on the bed unwrapped her child. She peered at the legs of her son, swathed in the thick napkin. Gingerly she lifted the corner, investigated what lay underneath.

'Got all his bits, has he?' she asked the two doctors doubtfully.

But they were paying her no attention.